Clandestine Affairs of the Heart

Jonathon's Destiny

James R. Youngblood

iUniverse LLC
Bloomington

CLANDESTINE AFFAIRS OF THE HEART
JONATHON'S DESTINY

This is a work of fiction. All of the characters, names, incidents, organizations, and dialogue in this novel are either the products of the author's imagination or are used fictitiously.

iUniverse books may be ordered through booksellers or by contacting:

iUniverse
1663 Liberty Drive
Bloomington, IN 47403
www.iuniverse.com
1-800-Authors (1-800-288-4677)

Because of the dynamic nature of the Internet, any web addresses or links contained in this book may have changed since publication and may no longer be valid. The views expressed in this work are solely those of the author and do not necessarily reflect the views of the publisher, and the publisher hereby disclaims any responsibility for them.

Any people depicted in stock imagery provided by Thinkstock are models, and such images are being used for illustrative purposes only.

Certain stock imagery © Thinkstock.

ISBN: 978-1-4917-0154-6 (sc)
ISBN: 978-1-4917-0155-3 (hc)
ISBN: 978-1-4917-0156-0 (e)

Library of Congress Control Number: 2013913689

Printed in the United States of America.

iUniverse rev. date: 8/9/2013

Table of Contents

I awoke but I couldn't see anything. It was so dark it was pure blackness. I tried to get up but couldn't move. I felt weird. I felt a sense of being under water. It was as if I were in a whirlpool that was twisting my body and pulling me down deeper and deeper. I struggled to swim but couldn't move. As I struggled, my thoughts went back to my childhood in the swimming pool with Mom and Dad. I remembered Dad always said, "If you relax your body, you will float to the top. When your head gets out of the water, you can breathe."

Mom would throw me to Dad and he would let me sink and then pull me up. Dad would then throw me back to Mom. She let me sink a little before she pulled me up. They said I would come up out of the water laughing. I remembered that I really liked swimming. I never had a fear of water. Maybe this was the reason.

I wasn't laughing now. I was afraid. *"This is weird. What the fuck is going on? Where the hell am I? I've got to get my ass out of here."* I thought.

Then I became unconscious.

I woke again but stayed in a state of semi-consciousness. I don't know why, but my thoughts returned to my childhood. I tried to clear my mind but couldn't. I didn't know where I was. Hell, I didn't even know who I was.

I thought, *"If I could remember my name, I might remember everything. Who am I?"*

All of a sudden I remembered. My name is Jonathon Anthony Roberts Jr. I was born January 28, 1977 in San Diego, California. My Dad was a career naval officer, and my Mom was a homemaker.

The next memory that came to mind was the story of the Robert family's naval tradition and William Roberts, the first man in the Roberts family to be in the Navy.

Dad would tell the story and always concluded with, "William was the first in a line of naval Roberts that continues unbroken to this day.

You will become the next Roberts in the Navy, and you will go to the U.S. Naval Academy in Annapolis, Maryland." This story would be repeated over and over again throughout my life.

I remember mom and dad telling me that I was born blessed in three ways: "You have a photographic memory, you are a gifted athlete, and have the ability to easily learn foreign languages."

As I grew older, my interests turned to sports, science fiction, and anything water related. I was a swimmer while still in diapers, snorkeled by age five, and was a certified scuba diver by age nine. Mom and Dad always supported and encouraged my interest in sports.

I remembered standing in front of a large map on the wall. The map had colored pins all over it. I was tracking Dad's assignments and movements, at least the ones he could tell us about. I put red pins everywhere Dad had been deployed. I put yellow pins in the places we had traveled and, finally, blue pins in the places we had lived.

I remembered we moved around and traveled a lot when I was young. This gave me the opportunity to learn languages and cultures. I found that fascinating and educational. Traveling developed a love of world cultures and history.

This lifestyle continued until I started high school. Dad was able to get an assignment in San Diego that would permit my sister and me to go through high school uninterrupted. We had finally stopped moving.

We moved to Coronado, California in August, 1992. I started high school there and soon met Kimberly Lorraine (Kim) Barnett.

Kim was petite and had a fabulous smile; in fact, she was always smiling. Kim was a girlie girl. She was non-athletic with average intelligence.

Kim didn't socialize much. She just hung around with me. We were great buddies and were inseparable.

Even though we didn't really date, everyone assumed we were a couple. This, as it turned out, destroyed any chance of my dating other girls. I wanted and tried to date, but all the girls thought I was trying to cheat on Kim. Consequently, I got an unjustified reputation as a womanizer and cheat.

It didn't really bother me because I was consumed with preparing myself to becoming a Navy SEAL.

In addition to everything else I was involved with, I joined the Sea Scouts. I achieved Quartermaster, the equivalent of Eagle Scout, and learned close order drill.

One day at school in the beginning of the 11th grade, I saw a guy pulling at Kim's arm trying to drag her. I ran up, pushed him away, and drew back to hit him.

Kim yelled, "Stop, it's OK. This is George Edwards.

He is new here, and we were just kidding around."

"Sorry," I said, and we shook hands.

This is the day George Arthur Edwards came to Coronado High School. George was about my size, athletic, and good looking. We hit it off and immediately became close friends. Now there were three of us, and we were inseparable.

One day, I told George of my plans to go to Annapolis and become a Navy SEAL.

George said, "I have ideas about going into the Air Force and becoming a fighter pilot."

I said, "Why not go into the Naval Academy with me. If you want to be a pilot, why not be the best. That could only be done by becoming a Navy pilot."

George asked, "Why do you think Navy pilots are the best?" I said, "They have to do everything the Air Force pilots have to do, but then, a Navy pilot has to fly those planes on and off a thousand foot moving runway. That takes a higher level of skill than being an Air Force pilot." We both debated it over the next couple of years. I finally convinced George to apply for the Naval Academy.

Soon after school started, we discovered that we were all Star Trek fans. I adopted the role of Spock, George was Captain Kirk, and Kim was Uhura. I had a vivid imagination and pictured myself exploring the universe with Captain Kirk.

Throughout high school, the three of us read everything written by Jules Verne, Ray Bradbury, and Carl Sagan.

Speaking of books, I had my own special book. The book was "The Greatest Salesman in the World" by Og Mandino. My Dad gave it to me on my 15th birthday. He said I was now old enough to understand it.

This book gave me my life's motto, *"Failure will never overtake me if my determination to succeed is strong enough."* I truly believe in this motto.

I woke again remembering my motto. I began repeating it and thinking, *"If I believe this, I'll find a way to get out of this predicament."*

I went out again.

I don't know if I was awake or dreaming. I was again remembering George and Kim in high school. It was becoming obvious that Kim and George had feelings for each other. It was also obvious that George wasn't going to make a move on her because he thought Kim and I were a couple.

With this in mind, I took George aside and said, "George, I think Kim likes you." George sort of hung his head down and said, "How do you know?" I replied, "It's obvious. I think you should ask her out."

"Isn't she your girl?" George asked. I said, "No, we are just buddies."

George replied, "Wow, I will."

Then I told Kim that I thought George liked her.

She said, "I like him, too, but he has never made a move."

I said, "I think he just might ask you out. You two should date."
Kim said, "We'll see."

That same day George asked Kim for a date, and they started dating exclusively.

George and Kim were now a couple, and I felt awkward. I wanted a girlfriend, but my "cheating" image still kept me alone. Awkward or not, we remained the three musketeers.

My hormones were now in a serious rage, and I wanted to date but the same "cheating" image was still dogging me.

At last there was hope for me on the dating front. After it became obvious that George and Kim were a couple, several girls began coming around.

One girl in particular, Jennifer Albertson, showed interest in me, and I immediately asked her for a date. She said yes and we began to date regularly.

Jennifer did not sleep around, but she soon let me know she loved sex. Of course, I had no problem with that. After a couple of dates, we had sex for the first time.

I was so clumsy that I was embarrassed. Clumsy or not, I liked it and it didn't seem to bother Jennifer.

She tried her best to become the fourth Musketeer but just couldn't. She just couldn't deal with our active routine. This was, mostly, because she had nothing in common with us.

Our dedication to mental and physical development simply overwhelmed Jennifer, and she finally broke up with me.

We were only status symbols for her because George and I were popular athletes. This became a common theme with girls and me throughout high school.

One problem was that George and I always talked about nothing but sports or what we were going to do after high school.

Kim always seemed to be genuinely interested in whatever we said or did and was always there. Other girls weren't very interested.

George and I did everything together and lettered in the same sports. I set school records in track and field, distance, and cross country events. In fact, I wasn't even challenged. I was also the quarterback on our varsity football team.

George, Kim, and I studied together all through high school. We developed a routine where we always challenged everything and each other. One of us would always play the Devil's Advocate.

This helped us graduate as straight "A" students.

In the summer before our senior year, George and I decided to join the local Iron Man Triathlon Club.

The San Diego Iron Man Club was made up of Navy, Marines, and a few civilians. Since we were only seventeen, we had definitely met our matches. It was very clear that we were out of our league, but that didn't deter us.

Both of us, at the beginning, were consistently dead last in every event.

After a while, I finally moved from next to last to third from last. As the weeks went on, I steadily rose in rankings until I finished third in the last event before I went to the Naval Academy.

During my year on the Iron Man Team, I became friends with Alfred (Al) Smith, one of the youngest SEALs.

When I would become frustrated by not finishing higher, Al told me that my body was still developing so I shouldn't worry. After all, I was only seventeen years old. That not only helped me stay motivated, it gave me self-confidence.

The most important thing for me was that I was performing better than guys who were already Navy SEALs. In my mind, this proved I would make SEAL.

I went on to graduate Valedictorian of my high school class.

My thoughts returned to the present. Someone was removing straps from my arms. The instant the straps were off I started swinging wildly trying to hit whoever was there. Two guys with big strong hands held me and sat me up. A third guy put some kind of belt around my waist. Then, he put shackles on my wrists and secured them to the belt. Next, he put shackles on my ankles.

During all of this I tried to fight them. I lashed out but couldn't touch them. A man said, *"Boy, this guy is a fighter, and strong too! We'll have to juice him some more. Just give him enough to calm him. We want to keep him awake."*

I felt the needle go into my arm but felt nothing after that.

I felt much like the first time I awoke. I was in a fog, drifting in and out of consciousness. While in this dreamlike state, I remembered that I was in the US Naval Academy.

I remembered heading to the U.S. Naval Academy still obsessed with becoming a Navy SEAL. What a new milestone in my life! I was now an adult, on my own, and filled with mixed emotions. My life up to now had been very good. I thought about becoming a SEAL.

SEAL duty would be high risk and require my undivided attention for at least the first five years. Considering everything, I believed it would not be right to subject a wife or girlfriend to this risk and sacrifice.

Therefore, I decided I would not marry or get into a serious relationship until I completed SEAL service. I would devote myself completely to my studies and physical conditioning. I aimed to exceed each of the Navy SEAL requirements.

I was now leaving home for good, so Mom and Dad decided they would accompany me for Induction Day or I-Day. The Navy encouraged family to attend I-Day.

On one hand, I was glad to be free of the nest, but, at the same time, it was a little scary and overwhelming. After all, I had spent my entire life preparing for this moment.

Oh well, here I am, now I've got to focus on the next four years. From what everyone says, the Naval Academy will be no walk in the park.

They say the freshman year is the hardest. This is the time the upper classmen try to harass new people into the Navy way. It is also said they weed out the weak ones by getting them to quit.

I feel confident that nobody will ever run me out. I felt that I could handle any harassment they would dish out. Beyond this, I didn't have a clue as to what is coming my way. I just know that many have gone before me successfully, so I am sure I can do it.

We boarded the plane, settled in. Shortly after we were airborne, I fell asleep. The next thing I knew the flight attendant was making the announcement that we were preparing to land.

Mom, Dad and I arrived at Baltimore International Airport and headed straight to Annapolis.

I reported to the Academy's Alumni Hall on I-Day, the first day of Plebe Summer.

As I walked to Alumni Hall, I couldn't help but notice how the buildings looked and how well the grounds were kept. Other than that, everything about the campus seemed intimidating.

Arriving at Alumni Hall, we received our first orders which were given quickly, loudly and sternly. They were, "From now on, the first and last words out of your mouth will be 'Sir' or 'Ma'am,' do you understand?"

Everyone yelled in unison, "Yes sir!"

We then surrendered our civilian clothing and personal belongings. We were then sent for a haircut and medical screening which included drug and alcohol testing.

After these things were completed, we went to our dormitory and then to Tecumseh Court where we were sworn in and signed our "Oath of Office" papers.

Following the swearing-in, we were allowed to briefly visit with family and friends.

The time with family was so short that it didn't seem worth attending.

I, however, appreciated their being there because we would not be allowed to meet with family again until the end of Plebe Summer in mid-August.

I entered the dorm room and heard, "What kept you?"

It was my best friend George.

I replied, "Looks like you and I are my roommates."

My Dad was very well connected and was able to get recommendations for George to the Naval Academy.

I was glad George was here because our lives were about to change forever. We could help each other like we had always done.

I wondered out loud, *"How tough will it be here? Will we be OK?"*

I had many other questions, but I quickly fell back on my motto, *"Failure will never overtake me if my determination to succeed is strong enough."*

In fact, I fell back on my motto many times in the Plebe year and it always gave me the will and strength to handle whatever they dished out.

George and I continued studying together throughout the Academy.

Kim elected to go to the University of Baltimore to be near George, and we all spent our free times together as soon as we were allowed to.

Sometimes Kim brought a date for me, but my life wasn't conducive to a regular relationship.

Both George and I were on the Academy swimming and football teams.

Having been the quarterback in high school, I was surprised when they decided that I would play free safety.

As it turned out, I was well suited for the position.

As a quarterback in high school, I learned to lead the team.

This quarterback experience gave me the skills to be the defensive leader, and, since I thought like a quarterback, I was pretty good at reading the opponent's offense.

It also had the side benefit of better physical conditioning as it related to SEAL training.

I also decided to join the precision drill team.

The drill team taught me to discipline my entire body.

I had to pay attention to every small detail, from head to toes, muscle control, hand eye coordination and, especially, learned how to feel my piece (rifle).

I could throw and twirl my piece blindfolded.

Both of us spent as much extracurricular time as possible preparing ourselves for meeting the SEAL physical requirements.

We wanted to make sure we could exceed every requirement to the maximum extent possible.

I met the physical requirements relatively easy where George had to struggle just to meet them.

I encouraged and pushed George every day until he exceeded all the requirements.

We felt ready for what laid ahead.

Because George and I were so well prepared, we took everything in stride. As a consequence, the Academy was easier for us than most.

The Abduction

ow I was fully awake and remembered everything. My mind immediately came to the present. I remember it was the end of my second year at the US Naval Academy and I decided to stay on campus for the summer and study. Since I was first in my class, I wanted to get a head start on my junior year. It would also give me some time to explore a little of the surrounding area.

One sweltering August afternoon the air was dead calm, with not even a breeze. The temperature and humidity both were in the high nineties.

My Godfather, Bill O'Leary, had called and said he wanted to take me to dinner.

It was a very quiet day on campus, so I just laid around in my room and studied. At least I had air conditioning and that helped a lot.

Around 1600, I heard a knock on the door. I answered the door, and Bill, in his usual Irish manner, said, "Hey laddie, let's celebrate. I'm buying."

"Hi Bill, it works for me. It's good to see you. How's Cindy?" I replied.

"She's great!" he said.

I grabbed my hat, and we left. It was a welcome relief to get out with good company. It really made my day. We had dinner at the Inner Harbor and caught each other up on everything and everybody.

After dinner, Bill said, "Let's have a couple of drinks before we call it a night."

I said, "OK" and we stopped at a sports bar.

I drank a couple of beers, and Bill had his usual. It was a Tulamore Dew in a stone crock served in a water glass—straight up, no ice. I'm surprised that they even knew what that drink was, much less having the stone crock.

We left the bar to return to the dorm. When we got outside, there was a crowd milling around outside the bar. As we worked our way through the crowd, someone bumped hard against my shoulder. I felt something like a pin prick. I rubbed it, and, thinking nothing of it, kept on walking.

A couple minutes later, I began to feel dizzy. My eyes seem to fog up. Something very strange was happening to me. My legs were getting wobbly, and I reached out to grab Bill's arm. Then I staggered and fell.

I was still in a fog, but I do remember Bill yelling out, "call 911."

The next thing I knew was that an ambulance arrived. I was on the brink of passing out, but I remembered being put on a gurney and the ambulance driving away. Then I passed out.

I awoke, and my mind was back in the real world.

I remembered I was shackled. A man said, "Welcome back to the world. Walk this way."

I replied, "Fuck you. I'm not going anywhere."

I tried to hit and kick them, and two more guys came and each grabbed one of my legs. The four of them carried me a short distance and stopped. I don't mind saying that I was scared.

I thought, *"Who the hell are these guys? I don't have any enemies. Do they have the wrong guy?"*

My mind was racing to understand what was happening to me and why.

We entered a door.

The room was very dark. All I saw were two strips of lights stretched in front of me. I had the feeling I was in a theater. The aisle lights were shining on both sides. Toward the front of the room, about where the first row would be, there was a table with a small spotlight illuminating the tabletop. About halfway to the table was a spotlight shining from the floor upward. We stopped at this small spotlight when it illuminated my face.

I thought, *"This is weird shit. Am I dreaming? Yes, that's it. I'll wake up in a little while and have a laugh about it."*

Deciding it was a dream, I relaxed and actually began to look forward to what would come next.

Just then, a mechanically-generated voice emanated from a speaker at my feet and said, "Please be seated." I felt something touch the back of my legs. The guys holding me forcibly pushed me into a chair. All of a sudden I realized this was not a dream. Now I was really afraid! My adrenaline began to increase, and I thought, *"I've got to figure out how to get out of this damned place. But how?"*

Before I could do anything, they strapped my arms and legs to the chair.

The voice said, "Sorry we have to do this, but we've had a few bad situations by people freaking out and hurting themselves—just like you've been doing."

I thought, *"Damn! I'm in deep shit now. They must be going to torture me. But why? I'll try and convince them they have the wrong guy. Since I haven't seen anything, maybe they will let me go."*

Then one of the guys put a bottle of water in front of my face, and the voice said, "Drink some water and you'll feel better." I just said, *"Fuck you!"*

My attention went back to the table where there was what looked like a piece of paper and a pen.

My thoughts quickly returned to how I could convince them they had the wrong person. *"What could I possibly say?"*

Then the voice began to speak.

"Is your name Jonathon Anthony Roberts, Jr.?"

"Yes", I replied. *"Well, so much for convincing them they have the wrong guy. They didn't."*

"You have been brought here to discuss your future."

I thought, "*Well, at least they said I have a future. That made me feel better.*"

The voice continued, "Unfortunately, I can't give you many details unless you take an oath of secrecy.

I know you must be wondering what the hell is going on."

I said, "That's the understatement of the century!"

He continued, "Let me put your mind at ease. I want you to just hear me out. After I finish, you can leave or stay. You simply have to say no, and you will be released unharmed.

If you decide you want to hear more, all you have to do is swear an oath of secrecy. I will explain everything after you take the secrecy oath.

Further, I strongly advise you to take the oath and listen. This is a major turning point in your life, and you should be well informed before you make your decision. Do you wish to proceed or leave?"

I don't know whether I felt better or worse, but he definitely got my attention. I figured, *they haven't harmed me so far. What have I got to lose? They have me and can do anything to me they feel like doing. OK, I'll listen.*"

"I'll listen." I replied.

The voice asked, "Do you swear that you will never acknowledge that this meeting took place as well as everything said here?"

"Yes sir."

A hooded person wearing all black emerged from the shadows, picked up the paper a pen, and brought them to me. He or she held a small flashlight on the paper so I could read it. The voice then said, "Read and sign this secrecy oath."

I read the paper, signed it, and returned it to the person.

The voice then said, "You have been sponsored for entry into our little secret club. If you accept this assignment, you will, from this day forward, might be a member of our club."

I thought, "*Man, what a relief. I think I'm going to like this.*"

The voice continued, "From now on, regardless of assignments throughout your Navy career, you will be in the US Naval Intelligence Service.

The first thing you have to do is understand that you may, at any time, be called on for clandestine tasks outside of your regular duties. These assignments will be temporary. Your current bosses will only know that you have received orders from higher authority, and they are prohibited from asking questions about your temporary assignment. Even you won't know what your assignment is about until later. At completion of the assignment, you will be returned to your regular duty.

Next, the way we operate these assignments is that you will have only two contacts into the Service. You are never to discuss anything about the Service with anyone but your official contacts.

One contact will be your primary contact. He or she is the only person who will ever be authorized to give you orders or approvals. The other is your secondary contact.

If you cannot make contact with your primary, and it is absolutely necessary to do so, you may contact your secondary. At that time, your secondary becomes your primary. Subsequently, he or she will give you a new secondary.

The only time your secondary will ever initiate contact with you is when your primary becomes incapacitated. Again, your secondary becomes your new primary.

All commands, orders, and communications are verbal only. Is that understood?"

"Yes sir."

"We see that you have wanted a naval career from early childhood. Is that correct?"

"Yes sir."

"Just so you know that we know you better than you know yourself, we know that, in the ninth grade, you came to the rescue of a girl who was fending off unwanted advances from the school bully. You the beat him badly but then became friends."

"Yes sir, how did you know that?"

The voice said, "I told you we know everything. We even know how often you jack off.

15

We also see that you are fluent in Chinese, Russian, German, French, Spanish, and Italian with some knowledge of Arabic and Hebrew.

We know you have been gifted with a photographic memory.

These are personal attributes that makes you important to the Service and the reason you have been sponsored.

Are you also prepared to accept and carry out extremely hazardous assignments?"

"Yes sir."

After a pause, the voice said, "In that case, we have an offer to make you. The offer, however, has conditions that are both absolute and extreme.

Before we make the offer, you will have to trust that we have your future in mind and know that we will always consider your future along with the interest of the government. Is this acceptable?"

"Yes sir."

"Good.

First, we offer the following:

+ We will assign you to SEAL school.
+ After entering SEAL training, you will be sent to a special total immersion school to learn another foreign language.
+ You will then return to regular SEAL training.
+ After completion of your SEAL training, you will undergo mission specific training.
+ Following mission specific training, your assignment will be for an extended period of time.
+ You will then be assigned to Special Forces.
+ After your SEAL career, you will be sent to a major university to earn a Master's degree in Computer Science and a PHD in Linguistics.
+ You will then be fully prepared for the balance of your naval career.
+ Given all this, you must pledge to remain unmarried for five years and to have no serious personal relationships.

Is this understood?"

I hesitated for a moment thinking, *"Man, what a twist, but I immediately knew my answer would be yes. Now I'm glad this isn't a dream."*

"Yes sir." I replied.

"Is this career plan acceptable?"

"Yes sir."

"The conditions are:

1. You must graduate in the top twenty in your class at the Naval Academy.
2. You must become a SEAL.
3. You will be given a second identity as James Otis Duncan.

     The real James Duncan has no living relatives. He was recently killed in a clandestine operation in Kosovo. His records will not show his death. You will become him.

     This second identity will stay with you until you leave the intelligence service or the identity is compromised. At such time, James Otis Duncan will officially be killed.

     From now on, this identity must live where you live and travel where you travel.

     Wherever you live, you will set up an address at a 'Mailbox Etc.' or a similar business. You will then get a driver's license and set up a bank account with a credit card.

     In order to have a traceable history, you must regularly use the Duncan identity credit cards wherever you travel, rent a car, or use a motel or hotel. Also, use the Duncan credit card regularly for restaurants. In this way, records will show Duncan exists.

     By doing this, you will know the details of living and traveling because you actually experienced them.
4. You will also be given a foreign identity at some time in the future.

5. Immediately upon graduation, you will assume the identity of James Otis Duncan and travel as a civilian until you report for SEAL training.

"Failure to meet any condition will, automatically, void this contract, and you will be removed from this program and the Intelligence Service forever.

Do you understand and accept these conditions?"

"I understand and accept," I replied.

The voice had a thick document handed to me and said, "Read and sign this contract. It covers everything we promised and represents your agreement and acceptance. Take your time, but we would like to complete this before lunch.

At that time, you will have lunch with your primary contact. By the way, your contact is also the one who sponsored you into this program."

It took me about an hour to finish reading the contract. When I was done, I signed it. Now I was ready to meet my sponsor.

The voice said, "Good, now meet your sponsor."

After about a minute, both spotlights turned off and different indirect lights slowly turned up. The lights stopped increasing as soon as it became just light enough to leave the room. Then a figure emerged from the shadows.

A familiar voice said, "Interesting, huh?"

As he approached, the sponsor picked up the small spotlight and pointed it to his face. It was my Godfather Bill.

He removed the shackles and cut the straps off my arms and legs and only said, "OK, we'll leave now."

We went to the rear of the room and then down a very dark corridor to another door. It was eerie.

I'm thinking, *"This cloak and dagger stuff seems extraordinarily complex, but, I guess, they know what they are doing."*

We left the building and walked directly into a van which had its doors open. The van was backed close enough to the building that the doors touched the building. I guess it was to block my view. As soon as we got inside the van, the doors were closed behind us.

Bill then turned on the dome lights, and we sat on the floor of the van and talked. Bill filled me in on many things that would, one day, become my way of life.

As he talked, my mind tried to take in all the things he was saying. I only knew one thing for sure—my life would certainly change.

Bill told me that he and my father had been in this business their entire career. That's why we lived in so many places for relatively short periods.

Bill said, "*Your Dad thought you would excel in the Secret Service because your abilities were rare. So you see, you were always groomed for this job from your birth.*"

I wondered, "*How could Dad kept all this a secret? Would I be able to adequately learn multiple secret identities much less keep them straight in my mind? Did I even want it or was I simply brainwashed? I believe I want it.*"

In any event, the thought of it was exciting, and I looked forward to it. I was definitely hooked.

After about two hours, we stopped and transferred to a car. The windows were tinted such that I couldn't see out.

I thought, "*I have absolutely no idea of where we have been or anything except the shackles, the table, the spotlight, and inside the back of the van. These guys sure know how to do spook things.*"

We rode for another hour and then transferred to yet another car. After another hour, we stopped. We got out of the car, and I saw that it was a black SUV.

We were back at the Inner Harbor in downtown Baltimore.

Bill said, "It's nice to have you with us. You have to find your own way back to the Naval Academy." He then drove away.

After I got back, and for many days afterward, my mind raced with thoughts about what lay ahead beyond SEAL training.

I knew that Bill would remain a part of my life forever. My thoughts drifted back in time to Bill and his wife Cindy.

Bill was the personification of an Alpha male and the guy you wanted by your side in any tough situation.

Bill is a typical Irishman with a ruddy complexion, rusty red hair, and piercing blue eyes. A great story teller—some were even true. Like most Irishmen he never really got a suntan. He defined an Irish suntan as mostly covering up the blue veins. Quick with a joke . . . not the stand-up kind, but a funny comment about people, places or activities. He once told a waitress in tight jeans that she looked like "two cats in a bag, fighting to get out!"

Bill's wife, Cindy, was a Korean woman, who was born in Seoul, Korea, but came to New York when she was 7 years old. Bill loves dark haired, exotic women with dark eyes.

Her father was a Korean diplomat and settled in New York City.

Cindy was educated at NYU. She was very smart and could hold her own with Bill in any give and take. She has a great sense of humor and Bill thought she was the most beautiful woman he had ever seen. Bill would die for her.

He stood 6 feet three inches tall and weighed 220 pounds. He was very well built and strong as an ox. He had a great personality and was always full of fun. He looked anything but a naval officer.

Bill and Cindy were cut from the same cloth. Both were pranksters to each other and always kept everyone laughing at them or with them.

To this day, they acted as if they were on their honeymoon. They had no children and lived in an upscale apartment high rise near downtown San Diego.

During the times Bill was home, he and Cindy would, once every month or two, take my sister and me somewhere. It would be "our day" with the O'Learys. We would go bowling, to the zoo, movies, or somewhere cool. We were their substitute kids.

Also, about once a month the O'Learys would come to our house for barbeque, dinner, or a party. They never came empty handed. Bill would always bring something to drink, and Cindy would bring something she cooked or baked. Those were great times.

Reflecting on those days, I now realized that my father recognized my capabilities very early in my life. He gradually prepared me for my future life.

Dad felt God had given me special talents that were perfect for my planned life. I wondered just when my preparation really began.

"Do I really have my own desires? Can I think for myself? Or was I programmed to think only what my parents planted in my brain?"

I thought back to my earliest memories and decided that my destiny had been preordained by both family tradition and my parents before I was even born. I got so caught up in my mental journey that I couldn't think straight.

I thought, *"Man, what an ordeal this has been. It seemed to last far longer than a few hours.*

I spent the rest of the summer studying, swimming, and working out. It was a nice change of pace.

During the summer break, I was so relaxed that I didn't have the will to harass the Plebes. I actually encouraged a couple of guys that were having a hard time adjusting. I gave them my motto and told them to believe in it.

When I received my class assignments for Fall semester, I immediately saw that several of my optional classes had been substituted with new ones.

These new classes were selected for me. This trend would be with me throughout my career.

It had been a great journey getting to this point in my life. I loved the Naval Academy and was looking forward to my final two years. Now I tried my best to put all this out of my mind.

The next year at the Academy went by quietly with no further contact with Bill. I remained at the top of my class and found everything getting easier.

On the first day of our senior year, George and I were called to the Commandant of Midshipmen's Office.

The Commandant was USMC Colonel Jack Anderson.

Entering his office he said, "Be at ease, gentlemen.

I called you here to meet you personally.

I served with your fathers.

Jon, do you remember me?"

"No, sir," I replied.

"Well, my wife and I were at your house when you were around seven years old.

Your fathers and I were part of the Grenada Operation, Urgent Fury, in 1983.

My wife and I would like to invite you to our home for dinner this Friday night. Can you make it?"

George and I both, simultaneously, replied, "Yes, sir."

I said, "It would be an honor, sir."

George added, "I would consider it a privilege, sir."

The Colonel then said, "Very good, see you around 1800 hours. You may now return to your class."

George and I arrived at the Colonel's home at precisely 1800 hours and rang the doorbell.

His wife opened the door and said, "Hello, I'm Nancy Anderson. Come in."

We both said, "Very pleased to meet you, Mrs. Anderson."

"Please call me Nancy," she replied.

We went in and sat on the couch.

Just then Colonel Anderson came in and said, "Good evening gentlemen. Can I get you something to drink? Wine, beer, or something else?"

We both stood and said, "Beer, please, sir."

The Colonel asked, "I have Coors, Coors Light, and Guinness. Which shall it be?"

I said, "Guinness, thank you, sir."

George said, "Coors Light, sir."

Colonel Anderson began, "Dinner will be around 2130. That will give us time to get better acquainted."

Just then, Mrs. Anderson joined us and said, "Jack and I know both your parents and really wanted to meet you.

It isn't often we have sons of friends here."

The Colonel then talked about where he had served with our fathers, and Mrs. Anderson told some stories about things the wives did as a group.

The Colonel said, "I talked to both your fathers, and we have agreed that they will stay at our house while they are here.

We have also agreed that we will celebrate your graduation at our home. I hope you don't mind."

George and I both said, "That would be great, sir."

Then Mrs. Anderson said, "Jon, I understand you have other family members that served in the Navy."

I replied, "Yes, ma'am."

The Colonel then asked, "Didn't your grandfather also graduate from the Academy?"

I replied, "My grandfather, my great grandfather, and my great-great grandfather were Academy graduates."

George chimed in, "Jon is being modest. He knows the entire line of naval men in his family.

He even knows the story of the very first Roberts that started the line."

Mrs. Anderson quickly asked, "Tell us the story, Jon."

The Colonel and George both jumped in saying, "Tell it."

I said, "OK, you asked for it" and began.

"The first naval man in our family was William Henry Roberts.

He was born on August 10, 1560 to Ann Roberts, a prostitute, living over a bar where she plied her trade to the sailors.

He was a young street urchin in the seaport of Liverpool, England.

Ann had no idea who William's father was.

Ann Roberts would work all night and sleep all day leaving William to fend for himself. He was never supervised or cared for.

He seemed to always be hungry.

He would beg money from sailors and scrounge for food anywhere he could find it.

William grew up listening to sailor's tales of exploits in the foreign ports they visited.

The sailors seemed to always have lots of money to spend.

He thought, *"I'll be a sailor someday."*

William would spend all his time looking out at sea watching the ships anchored in the bay and those coming and going.

He especially liked to watch the sun go down when there was no fog.

Then he could clearly see the horizon and the stars which shined brightly.

He wondered; *"Where did they go? It must be exciting."*

Then he watched the sailors coming ashore in small boats.

"Someday, I will be a sailor," he again promised himself.

When William was twelve years old, a sailor moved in with his Mom and him.

This guy, Jacob, and William became close, and Jacob told William all about the Royal Navy and life as a sailor.

One day, William asked Jacob, "How old do you have to be to go into the Navy?"

Jacob said, "Well, the youngest they take would be thirteen years old as a Powder Monkey."

"What's a Powder Monkey?" William asked.

Jacob told him, "A Powder Monkey is a small sailor that goes into the gunpowder magazine and brings the powder to the canons."

So, when William was thirteen, he joined the Royal Navy.

William went to sea as a Powder Monkey on one of the King's sailing ships.

William's career as a sailor in the King's Navy had begun.

Having spent his entire life around sailors, William already knew the Navy lingo.

He easily fit in with the crew and was quickly accepted.

For the first time in his life, William had plenty to eat, good clothes on his back, and structure in his life.

William loved his new life.

Thus he began the tradition of career seafaring Roberts.

The first of the Roberts to immigrate to the United States was Peter Frank Roberts.

Peter was a Captain in the British Royal Navy when he first came to the United States. Once here, he knew he wanted to immigrate.

He liked the individualist way of the Americans and the fact that the U.S. Navy was in its infancy.

Peter later applied for and received a commission of Commodore in the U.S. Navy in 1825.

He served on the sloop of war—USS Vincennes, the first American naval vessel to circumnavigate the globe.

Every son and their sons became links in a long line of naval men that goes unbroken to this very day."

Mrs. Anderson applauded and said, "That was fascinating. Thank you for sharing."

"My pleasure," I said.

Mrs. Anderson then said, "Well boys, it's time to eat."

We all got up and went to the dining room.

We sat down and a server appeared with a bottle of wine and poured each of us a glass of Burgundy.

Then servers brought plates for each of us.

On the plates were filet mignon, a baked potato, and a bean casserole.

It was a fantastic meal.

When we finished, an Amaretto on the rocks was served as an after dinner drink.

We finished the drink, and, not wanting to wear out our welcome, I said, "I think it's time to call it a night."

Everyone said their goodbyes, and George and I walked back to our quarters.

The rest of the senior year was relatively uneventful.

Special Orders

❧

At the end of my senior year, just before Commissioning (Graduation) ceremonies, I was given orders that directed me to report to the Commanding Officer at NAS Patuxent (PAX) River, Maryland on the following Saturday. I drove to the base and reported in.

After reporting, I was given sealed orders not to be opened until I was airborne. I thought, *"Well, Jonathon, here we go. You asked for it and now you're about to get it."* I was then escorted to the flight line and boarded a waiting chartered jet.

The first class section only had four men, and they were in civilian clothes. Going into the coach section, I saw that I was the only passenger. *"How weird"* I thought. I sat down and buckled up. The plane took off, and I anxiously opened my orders.

The orders read, "You are ordered to assume the new identity as James Otis Duncan, a computer engineer from Stanford University.

Personnel on board this aircraft will provide you with all necessary documents and provide details of your new identity including family, friends, and hobbies.

When you finish reviewing your orders, proceed to the first class section where your intense briefing will take place along with your assignment details."

I finished reading the orders and went to the first class section. I was motioned to a seat, and they began the briefing.

They gave me a complete dossier on my new identity, ID, driver's license, credit cards, and bank account with $10,000 in it. I even got pictures of my fictitious family members. These guys didn't forget anything.

My task now was to memorize every detail of my new persona and to push reality out of my mind completely. I had to become someone else. I settled in thinking about what had just happened. *"What have I gotten myself into? Oh well, that's in the future."*

Graduation

s graduation neared, I was happy but began wondering about SEAL training and what might follow. Now with a little time on my hands, I reflected on family and the fact that having a family of my own seemed out of reach. I felt a little sorry for myself but figured it was best for now given what lay ahead of me for the next five years or so.

Family, and even a female relationship, would just have to wait. *"Wait a minute,"* I thought. *I'll be twenty-seven before I can even start a serious relationship. How long would it take to meet someone?*

The more I thought about it, the more I didn't like it.

Was this my destiny? I accepted my fate and put such thoughts out of my mind.

I was ready for celebrating. George and Kim were to get married immediately following graduation, and I was George's best man.

The day before graduation I was in my room packing when there came a knock on my door.

I answered the door and an officer said, "You are wanted in Colonel Anderson's office immediately. I am to escort you there."

I got my hat and followed him. The pace was very fast, almost a jog. I wondered what the urgency was. The first thing that came to my mind was the CIA. I hadn't heard a word since my abduction two years ago.

I figured it was time the other shoe dropped so I wondered what would be next. Would I not be going to SEAL training?

I thought of all kinds of scenarios but came up with nothing.

I arrived at the Colonel's office and my escort opened the door and said, "Go right in."

As I walked into the office, Uncle Bill and Colonel Anderson were standing in front of the Colonel's desk. Now I was sure it was a CIA thing.

Both men, however, had serious looks on their faces making me wonder what was actually up.

Bill took my outstretched hand and pulled me to him in a bear hug. Bill then said, "Jon, I have very bad news.

There is no easy way to say this so I'll just tell you that both your parents were killed on takeoff in San Diego.

I felt as though I was hit in the chest with a sledge hammer. I felt so weak I thought my knees would buckle beneath me. At the same time, I was very confused.

How could that be possible? My mind went in so many directions that I became dizzy.

As my mind began to clear, I thought about my sister Elaine. My heart immediately went out to her because I knew how hard she would take this. She would be all alone.

I wondered, *"Should I resign from the Navy to take care of her? Could I resign?"*

All I wanted to do now was call her. No, she was supposed to be here for my graduation.

I wondered, *"Did she come?*

Why wasn't she on the plane with them?"

Now I was more confused than ever.

Bill then said, "I'll stay with you until you leave here.

By the way, Elaine and George's parents came on a commercial flight, and Kim is picking them up from the airport."

Colonel Anderson said, "Jon, Nancy and I would like you, Bill, and Cindy to stay with us until you leave.

George, his parents, and Kim will be there as well."

"I'd like that, sir," I replied.

Bill asked, "What do you have left to do today?" "I only have to finish packing," I said.

"Good, I'll go with you and help with your things."

Colonel Anderson then said, "You guys go on to the house whenever you wish. Nancy and the Edwards will be there waiting for you to arrive." I said, "Thank you, sir," and we left to go back to the dorm.

I finished packing, and we left for the Anderson's.

As we walked back, I looked at everything in sight, and it suddenly hit me that the campus was beautiful. I simply hadn't noticed it until I realized this would be the last time I saw it. This only added to the sadness of everything else that had happened. In order to get my mind off my sadness, I tried to think about what SEAL training would really be like. This didn't work very well, so I decided to try and not dwell on it. I would just take one day at a time.

I graduated first in my class from the Naval Academy on May 26, 1999 and was assigned to Navy SEAL training in San Diego, California.

It left me with a very heavy heart and a lot of mixed emotions.

All I could think about now was, *"Boy I'm really on my own."*

I had no family left except my sister Elaine, and all my plans were now up in the air.

Before I left, my orders were changed to included ten days leave to settle my parent's affairs and thirty days regular leave.

After the graduation ceremonies, I packed my personal belongings and took them to FedEx.

All I wanted to do now was to be with Elaine. We needed each other now more than ever before.

I had already shipped my Harley to California for storage.

One of the good things was that George and Kim were married on May 27th.

They had a military wedding, and I was George's best man.

Immediately after the wedding, we said our goodbyes.

George would go on to flight training in Pensacola, Florida, and I left for San Diego and the funeral.

The funeral service was to be held on June 2nd.

Knowing I always wanted to see Alaska, Mom and Dad had given me an 11-day Alaskan cruise as a graduation present.

Dad felt it would be a good way to get away from it all and relax before the rigors and isolation of SEAL training.

They not only gave me a cruise but they gave me the Penthouse Suite on Holland America's SS Volendam.

Dad knew I wouldn't have another chance for years to come.

Mom had also insisted that I pack something suitable for the formal dinner that is always held on cruises. In her memory, I packed my black tuxedo trousers and my white dinner jacket even though I figured I wouldn't go. Who knows, I might actually go if I was lucky enough to find someone unattached to go with me.

I then took a plane to San Diego. My sister, Elaine, had taken an earlier flight, and we met at the airport.

We discussed what should be done with the house and decided that we should keep the family home in Coronado.

Dad's insurance paid off the house and had enough left over to pay off everything Mom and Dad owed.

With the decision to keep the house, we had little to do to complete the family affairs. The next day Elaine and I began settling those affairs.

I was sure that I would eventually be stationed in San Diego over my career and could live there. In the meantime, Elaine would continue living there while she attended San Diego State University.

We first completed everything that needed my signature, and Elaine said she would handle everything else after I left.

I then changed the name on my cruise tickets to my alias, James Duncan. On June 6th, I left for Vancouver, Canada where the cruise ship departed.

The cruise was an 11-day Inland Passage cruise from Vancouver to Seward and Denali National Park, June 7th through June 17th.

The Cruise

Day 1

I arrived, boarded the ship, checked in and got my room key, dining room assignment and an array of cruise related stuff.

Mom and Dad had given me the penthouse suite. It had large floor to ceiling windows, a king sized bed, separate sitting area with a baby grand piano, dining room, mini bar, refrigerator, entertainment and music center and veranda with Jacuzzi, wet bar and lounge seating.

It just couldn't get better than this, I thought. I concluded it was a big waste for someone traveling alone; in fact, I figured it would only make the boredom worse.

After getting settled into my suite, I wondered why so many things were in the room when the ship had everything you might want outside the room. I speculated that the suite must be used, mostly, by newlyweds on their honeymoon.

Oh well, I relaxed and explored the entertainment and music center in the room. It had everything.

Since all my things were put away in the room, I decided to take a walk around the ship to get my bearings and to figure out what I was going to do to fill the time for the next 10 days. I thought, "Boy, this is going to be boring until the cruise is over."

But I started thinking about the Academy, the SEALs and my future as I always did. This kept my mind busy. I eventually made it to the dining room for my first meal aboard the ship. It was delicious, and I was beginning to think this cruise might be OK after all. At least it would be relaxing and the food was good.

After dinner, I made my way back to my room and went to bed. I soon fell asleep.

Day 2—At Sea

❧

I awoke at my usual 05:30 and was starving. *"This is bull shit. I'm on a cruise ship and can't sleep in?"*

Today doesn't hold much promise because it is a day of nothing but cruising all day. Oh well, I'll just have my shower and take a look around the ship.

It was a little too early for breakfast but I decided to walk around the promenade deck until breakfast was served. The cruise line gave the option of having breakfast in the dining room or on the promenade deck buffet.

Since my dining room table was reserved for the entire cruise, I figured I might as well check it out so I would know where my table was. I found my table and sat down.

I wondered what the people at my table would be like since we would be eating at the same table every meal. I hoped they were friendly.

People slowly began to arrive and introduce themselves.

Then I saw two young women walking into the dining room. The first one looked to be my age and was very good looking.

The other one looked a bit younger. In fact her hair was in a ponytail and she was dressed in loose fitting jeans, a big unrevealing top and sneakers. It was as if she had just left a school campus. Actually, she had a nerdish, introverted, look about her.

My first thought was, *"It sure would be nice if the older one came to my table."* She came toward the table and I was feeling pretty good. She walked right toward me but went right past me to another table.

The younger girl also headed my way. As she got closer, she looked older. In fact, she also looked about my age. She neared my table and sat down next to me.

As she sat down she said, "Hi, I'm Annie," in a low soft voice. Her voice was the kind that would be a perfect radio or television voice.

I said, "Hi, I'm Jim."

She wore no makeup but, actually, was rather good looking up close and seemed to be very nice. *"Maybe things were looking up. I can see myself spending time with her."*

Then I figured she was actually with someone who just didn't come to breakfast. I decided to sneak a look to see if she was wearing a wedding band. After a minute or two I saw that she had no rings on her fingers. *"Hope at last!"*

As the conversations started it was quickly established that this was also a very intelligent lady, with self-confidence, poise and class.

Everyone at the table began talking to each other. Soon Annie and I began to talk almost exclusively to each other. We were both oblivious to everyone else.

During our talk, I asked, "Annie, what made you come on this cruise alone?"

She said, "My mother gave it to me as a graduation present. I didn't want to come, but Mom argued that since I had nothing to do until grad school resumed, there were no excuses not to come. I finally agreed and here I am."

"Well, I'm glad you did," I replied.

We continued to talk and the next thing I knew the waiter was gently saying, "Pardon me, but would you mind letting us clean the table for lunch?"

I said, "I'm very sorry. We didn't realize what time it was." We had sat there talking from breakfast until almost lunch.

We left the dining room and strolled for a while. Then we had lunch at the promenade buffet.

After lunch, we decided to go swimming on the sun deck. We went to our rooms, changed into swimsuits, and returned to the sun deck to find each other.

I arrived first, got two chaise lounges, and ordered two iced teas.

When Annie approached, she was wrapped in a large towel.

She pulled off the towel and laid it on the chaise lounge.

When she did, she simply took my breath away. She was wearing a bikini and was built like a Greek Goddess.

She lay down next to me and we started talking again.

I just lay there looking at her. I couldn't take my eyes off her. I tried my best to not let her see me gawking but I'm reasonably sure she was aware. She was classy enough to not show it.

"How could someone so smart be so beautiful?" I wondered.

She looked so different from breakfast. It's amazing how baggy clothes can literally hide beauty.

We joked, laughed, talked, and again lost all track of time.

We learned a lot of little things about each other even though I couldn't reveal much truth about me.

We quickly discovered that neither one of us liked today's music except some country songs that were played. Our favorite music was the mellow rock from the sixties and seventies. Our favorite group was The Eagles. We both liked James Taylor and Carole King; in fact, we liked pretty much every song of that genre.

Before either one of us noticed, it was nearing dinner time.

Annie asked, "Are you getting hungry?"

I said, "I will be by the time we change."

We then went our separate ways to change into our clothes.

During dinner, we didn't talk much.

After dinner while we walked on the promenade deck, we heard some great music playing in a nearby lounge.

I asked, "Would you like to stop for a drink and listen to the music?"

She said, "I'd love to. It sounds great."

We found a table, sat down and I ordered drinks. We just looked out at the ocean. It was dusk and the setting sun was very picturesque.

Annie said, "Isn't that just beautiful?"

I said, "It sure is."

We sat there in silence until the sun had gone down.

I didn't dance very well, but I had a strong desire to hold her so I finally said, "Care to dance?"

She said, "Yes, I'd love to."

She was magnificent! She danced so well I actually felt that I could somehow dance all of a sudden.

She was graceful and seemed to follow my every clumsy move.

I was in heaven. For an instant, I remembered thinking how boring the cruise was going to be. *"Boy was I ever wrong about that."*

We sat down, ordered another drink, and I said, "You know, the first time I saw you walking toward my table I thought we would make a great couple."

Annie asked, "What made you think that?"

"Oh, that's easy. I could see our future together," I said.

"How can that be?" she asked.

"I don't know. I just had a vision," I said.

"That's a pretty good line," she laughed.

"Don't laugh. It's no line," I said.

"If you say so," she replied.

We then danced until it was pretty late.

When we first danced, I felt that Annie was a little tense and was avoiding being close. She, in fact, seemed to resist body contact at all.

Other than that we danced very well together.

I decided that I wouldn't pull her too close to me.

By the end of the night, I was totally smitten with this angel from heaven. Also, I could sense, or hoped, that she might be feeling the same way about me.

It was getting late again and Annie said, "I think it's time we called it a day, don't you?"

I said, "Yes, I guess so."

Then I asked, "Could I kiss you goodnight?"

"When the moon is blue cheese," she replied.

"Shall I take that as a no," I asked.

"You got that right," Annie said.

I then asked, "What are your plans for tomorrow?"

"Actually, I have none."

"Have you, by any chance, ever kayaked?"

"Yes, I have."

"Would you go kayaking with me?"

"Sure, I'd love it."

I smiled and told her, "Great! See you at breakfast at 06:30?"

Annie said, "Sure. Goodnight," and with that we went to our rooms.

I lay in bed and wondered about her for a long time.

I thought,

"Did she have brothers and sisters?

Where did she go to school?

What did she like and dislike?

Was she in a relationship?"

I made a vow to myself to ask her all these questions. I wanted to know everything about her.

Day 3—Ketchikan

We met on the promenade deck at 07:00 for breakfast. After breakfast, we went into Ketchikan and spent four hours kayaking Orca's Cove. It was spectacular.

"This girl is a trooper" I thought.

We had lunch and returned to the ship in late afternoon.

We went to our respective rooms. I showered, got dressed and turned on some music. I reflected on the day and marveled at Annie. *"This is my kind of woman. Is she perfect or what?"*

I've had men who couldn't keep up with me and Annie stayed right with me. She seemed to do it effortlessly. Next, I just lay on the couch picturing Annie in my mind. *"God, she is beautiful."*

I was enjoying my thoughts of her so much that I felt anger at the intrusion of my thoughts when it became time to go to dinner. On the other hand, I came to my senses when I realized I was going down to have dinner with her.

Timing was great. We met at the door to the dining room and went to our table together. Everyone was at the table when we arrived. After saying our hellos, we all talked about what everyone did on their excursions.

After dinner, Annie and I had gone to the rear of the ship where there was a sun deck overlooking the water.

We found chaise lounges that were positioned so that we could lie there and watch the ship's wake.

It seemed to go all the way over the horizon.

I finally said, "Tell me all about yourself. I want to know everything about you."

Annie said, "There's not much to tell. Besides that, it would be boring."

I said, "Tell me anyway, please. I promise not to be bored."

Annie said, "OK but don't fall asleep on me."

"Never," I said.

Then she began. "My name is Annie Harrison. I was born on May 3rd, 1978 in Oceanside, California.

My Dad was Marine Corporal and was killed in a training accident on August 12, 1978.

I have a step-dad and consider him to be my real dad. He raised me since I was two years old. He was a Captain in the Navy. After he retired we moved to Virginia Beach, Virginia. He died this past April."

"I'm sorry," I said.

Annie continued, "I graduated from High School in Virginia Beach. I played softball, ran cross country, and was on the swimming team."

"I just received my Bachelor's from MIT," she added. I will continue at MIT for my Master's and PhD."

I asked, "What will be your major?"

"I'll get my Master's in Business Management and haven't decided on my PhD."

After that, I will be going to work in the company founded by my dad.

Annie then said, "That's about all there is to know about me.

Now, it's your turn."

I thought, "What have I gotten myself into?

What can I say?"

I figured that I could tell her a lot without divulging anything that would compromise my secret side.

I said, "Well, here goes nothing."

My dad is a career naval officer, and I attended Coronado High School. I played football, baseball and track. I'm an avid swimmer and play golf and tennis.

I received a Bachelor's in Computer Science from Stanford University.

I currently live nowhere because, from here, I'm going into Navy SEAL training."

"That's great," she said.

"I've worked toward being a SEAL all my life, but it has a down side. I had to commit to five years of training and service, mostly overseas."

"That's my story, such as it is," I said.

We then continued to small-talk the time away.

We returned to our respective rooms to take off our coats before going to our favorite lounge.

Tonight, as we danced it was subtly different. The way Annie danced this time I felt maybe she was warming up to me. Her body felt great. I could feel her muscles but her body was not hard. It was soft and sensuous.

I held her a little tighter against me, and we took dancing to another level.

I don't know why but I've never danced better in my life. We moved as if we were one. It had to be Annie since I had two left feet before her.

I held her firmly and turned her to my left. As I did, her left leg slightly raised off the floor. My right leg slid a little farther between her legs than it usually did.

I then turned her back to my right, our legs still interlaced, and her legs squeezed my leg as she turned. Actually, she was simply hanging on for dear life. Never-the-less, we shivered and I knew that we both were feeling it.

That single dance broke down all stiffness and tension that was there until now. We danced for another hour and I walked Annie to her cabin.

I stood there looking into her eyes and said, "Good night," eager for a sign that she might let me kiss her good night. There were no such signs given, so I just said good night and went back to my cabin for to get some sleep. We agreed to meet on the promenade deck at 07:30 ready for our whale watching excursion.

Day 4—Juneau

I met Annie and we left the ship and took a boat to watch for whales in the morning. We got back and had a late lunch. After lunch, we spent the afternoon just wandering around Juneau and window shopped. It was a very nice leisurely afternoon.

As we walked, I couldn't help but notice that Annie looked very feminine but she is actually very athletic. I learned that she liked many outdoor activities and was a very good all-around athlete.

Back aboard ship, we had an early dinner and then attended a show in the theater. After the show, I walked Annie back to her cabin.

We picked up our conversation where we left off. It seemed so natural to do that. During our conversations, I told her that I had a penthouse suite.

She asked, "What is it like? I only have a small cabin and no window."

I described the suite and she said, "I can't believe they have anything that large on a ship."

I remarked, "You'd be surprised. Would you like to see it?"

"Sure," she said.

I showed her the suite, and Annie said, "I see it, but I still can't believe this."

I said, "Make yourself at home and put on some music while I change."

As I changed I heard a beautiful voice singing accompanied by a piano. When I came into the room I saw Annie at the piano. She was the voice I heard singing.

"My God, what can't this angel do?"

Annie stopped and I said, "Please don't stop."

Annie continued playing the piano while I just sat and watched her.

"Tonight I'm going to try kissing her goodnight,"

Finally, Annie said, "I think it's time for me to go."

I said, "OK, I'll walk you to your cabin."

At her door, I looked into Annie's beautiful eyes and leaned in to give her a kiss goodnight. Annie lifted her finger to my lips, "Not yet Jim, goodnight," she replied.

"OK, see you at breakfast?"

"I'll be waiting," Annie said.

Day 5—Skagway

We left the ship early and took the White Pass & Yukon Route Railroad tour. The railroad was built in 1898 during the Klondike Gold Rush. It was a narrow gauge railroad and an International Historic Civil Engineering Landmark, a designation shared with the Panama Canal, the Eiffel Tower and the Statue of Liberty. We were excited to be seeing it together.

After the train trip, we walked around Skagway for a while and returned to the ship.

I asked Annie, "How about coming to the penthouse until dinner? I'd like to hear you play the piano."

"That would be nice. I love the view from your room."

We stayed there until dinner. It was so relaxing to hear her play and sing.

I thought, *"A man sure could get used to this."*

I fixed us a drink and sat beside her at the piano. She then insisted that we sing together. After some arm twisting, I did the best I could.

It was very nice. I couldn't believe that I enjoyed singing with her. On the other hand, anything I did with Annie felt good.

We went to dinner and then to our favorite lounge. After a few dances we decided to get to bed early. We said our good nights, turned in, and I slept like a baby that night.

Day 6—The Formal Dinner Dance

A t breakfast the next morning, Annie asked, "Are you, by any chance going to the formal dinner dance tonight?"

I said, "Yes, but only if you will go with me."

She said, "Great. What are you wearing?"

I said, "I have black tuxedo trousers and a white dinner jacket."

"What color is your shirt?" she asked.

"Black," I replied.

Annie asked, "Do you mind if I buy you a different color shirt to wear?"

I said, "Tell me what color you want me to wear and I'll see if I can buy one."

Annie then said, "I would really like to pick it out. I don't want it to clash with my dress."

I said, "OK, if you really want to." "I'll pick you up at your room."

"By the way, I want to buy you a flower to wear. Is that appropriate and if yes, what should I get?"

She said, "Make it a white corsage to match your jacket.

By the way, I don't want you to pick me up. I'll meet you at the ballroom door.

I don't want you to hang around waiting for me and I don't want to be rushed," Annie insisted.

I said, "OK, see you there."

Before we finished breakfast, Annie said, "One more thing. We can't see each other again until dinner."

"Why not," I asked. She said, "I have too many girl things to do the rest of the day. See you tonight."

We separated and I was lost! Without Annie, I felt as though I had lost an arm and leg.

Being without her felt like what I'd heard drug or alcohol withdrawal was like. It was downright painful.

Having no guy things to do, I stayed in my room and thought about Annie all day. I pondered my life after the cruise.

If I hurt this much after a couple of hours away from Annie, how would I feel a day, week, or longer, without her? I tried to put the thought out of my mind but couldn't. Then my mind came back to reality.

I cursed that damned commitment.

I was to be away from Annie for at least five years and that was a simple fact. I just couldn't expect her to wait on the chance that I would even still be alive then.

I decided that I had to tell her that I was falling in love with her and that falling in love was a major problem under my current circumstances.

I felt she deserved to know the extent of my commitment on the chance she might be having similar feelings for me. I promised myself that I would tell her after dinner.

While I was killing time, there was a knock at the door. When I answered the door a busboy asked, "Mr. Duncan?"

I said, "Yes." He then handed me a shirt on a hanger and a box.

First, I opened the shirt. It was a Burgundy wine colored collarless shirt. I thought, "This is very nice."

Then, puzzled, I opened the box wondering what it could be. In it were a white silk cumber bun and a little button cover that you wore instead of a tie. It was a mother of pearl with a "V" set into black onyx and incased in a silver base. It was very classy and appeared to be expensive.

I thought, *"I just can't let Annie pay for this."*

I got dressed and I must admit, I had never looked so good because I would never have bought this color combination. It looked great. I attributed that to women having better taste than men.

I went to the ballroom, found the Captains table and sat down to wait for Annie. Once again, I found myself waiting and looking toward the front door.

The room began to fill and still no Annie. Then I could not believe what I saw at the entrance to the room.

I looked again to be sure that it really was Annie.

There she stood in a long cherry red silk evening dress.

The dress was slightly clinging to her body and gracefully embracing her breasts. It also showed a hint of her thighs beneath the dress as she moved.

The dress was wide at the top and was just enough off her shoulders to expose her long neck.

Her hair was down and fell just below her shoulders. Her hair was reddish auburn and gently caressed her shoulders. It seemed to glisten in the light as she walked. This was the first time she had not had her hair in a ponytail.

"She must have had it color enhanced. It seemed a little darker and a little richer."

The rear of the dress was open to her waist showing her bare back.

The dress was low cut in front conservatively showing just the right amount of cleavage.

She wore a red choker about two inches wide. The color of the choker matched the dress and it had two rows of tiny pearls around it. It was pure elegance.

Her dress was also split in front slightly exposing her legs as she walked.

Annie's nails were cherry red and she was wearing white, opened toed, high heels.

"*I've never seen such a transformation. This was a complete makeover.*"

She would put to shame any model on any fashion magazine or movie star attending the Oscar's.

This was not the same Annie I had been seeing. This was an elegant, sophisticated, and exquisitely beautiful woman.

I thought, "*Man, this isn't going to help me deal with losing her.*"

I quickly went to the door and escorted her to the table.

As Annie and I walked toward the table, every eye in the room was on her. I even heard women gasp.

I had never, in my life, felt so much pride. This lovely vision was actually my date.

My shirt, highlighted by the cumber bun, perfectly blended with her attire. When we were side by side, I was like a perfectly matched accessory designed to further show her off.

At this moment, I felt I was the luckiest and proudest man in the world.

As she walked slowly to the table, I began to think about the future without Annie because I was committed to leave her.

I thought, "*Should I abandon my commitments?*"

Then I remembered, "*Annie said she had commitments as well.*"

I was torn and it was killing me.

"*What did I do to deserve this?*"

After everyone was seated at their tables, the Captain announced, "On behalf of Holland America, I would like to welcome you all."

After the Captain's toast we dined and engaged in small talk with the passengers around us. As we sat there, I couldn't help being filled with emotions I never felt before. Here I was at the Captain's table with the most beautiful woman I had ever seen. I was overcome with peace and love for this woman.

Then reality hit me. This would soon come to an end, and I would never see her again.

"*Why did my life take such a twist?*"

I just had to push these thoughts out of my mind and focus on making the most of the little time we still had together. I took Annie's hand and led her to the dance floor and we danced the evening away.

As we were walking back to her room, I said, "There is something bothering me and I'd like to tell you about it."

"Let's change clothes and then I'll explain everything."

"Would you come to the penthouse? What I have to say must be said in absolute privacy."

Puzzled, she said, "OK," and left to change.

In about half an hour she knocked on the door and I opened it. She still looked great without the red dress.

I asked, "Will you play Rhapsody in Blue for me?"

"Sure," she said with a puzzled look.

I said, "Play it softly please."

She began to play and I poured us a drink. I just sat there staring at her.

Annie kept looking at me as she played. It was obvious that she was concerned.

I could almost see the gears turning in her brain trying to figure out what I was going to say.

When she finished the song, I motioned her to come to the couch. I took her hand and I started my explanation.

I began, "Annie, you first have to swear that what I am about to tell you will never be told to anyone, not even your mother."

Annie said, "I swear."

I told Annie, "I will tell you as much as I can without divulging secrets I am sworn to keep. You will have to trust me on the rest of it.

First, I am committed to a Navy career. I come from a very long unbroken line of career Navy men. Second, I have already had my education paid for by the Navy, and I'm going to SEAL training from here. Third, I already have an overseas assignment that will keep me away for at least five years." Further, I said, "It is a very high risk volunteer assignment."

Annie said, "I don't really understand but I'll try."

Then, I said, "I'm falling in love with you, and I don't want to chance hurting you if you might be having feelings for me."

She said, "I am feeling the same way about you.

I think we both have a big problem. I also have previous commitments, and I'm having the same trouble dealing with it."

"Boy, in a way, I'm relieved that Annie understands. On the downside, both of us are going to have to deal with it now. Well, what's done is done."

We talked about the situation we were in and about what we should do about it from here. We both agreed that we had to go our separate ways after the cruise.

I then said, "I want you to be free to go on with your life. I think the best thing to do is to not keep in touch. That way, it will be more definite and make it easier to put it behind us. If it is meant to be, we will somehow find each other again."

Annie, reluctantly, agreed.

After continuing to play for a while, Annie said, "Jim, can you make a Cosmo?"

I made the drink and brought it back to the piano.

Annie then said, "Let's go out to the veranda." I followed her and she stood there looking up at the sky.

The sky was clear and millions of stars made a magnificent backdrop for the moon. It was the first night of the full moon.

"What a glorious sight," I said.

"Yes, it is," Annie replied.

We just stared at the night for a few minutes.

"I want you to know this has been the most wonderful evening of my life," I said.

"Yes, it was for me too," Annie replied.

As I looked at the moon, it appeared to have a bluish tint.

I said, "I've always heard about a blue moon, but this is the first time I've ever seen one."

Annie then moved close and whispered softly into my ear, "I think it's the cheese."

"Wow, could this be the signal?" I hoped.

I decided I would chance it. I said nothing but then looked into her eyes and slowly bent down and very gently kissed her lips. It was very nice and I felt warm all over.

Annie did nothing for a few seconds, and then she put both her arms around my neck, her body slightly brushing against me, and kissed me back.

I again, looked into those beautiful eyes, waited for a few moments, then pulled her firmly against me and we kissed each other with passion this time. It felt like an electric shock ran from my toes to my head. My legs trembled like they did when I was thirteen.

The fourth of July fireworks were only child's play compared to the fireworks that went off inside of me.

"My God, I've kissed other girls before but I've never felt like this in my entire life," I thought.

"Oh, how wonderful you are," I told her.

She said, "I think you are wonderful, too."

I looked into her beautiful eyes and whispered, "I love you."

Annie said, "Oh Jim, I love you, too."

A little while later I said, "Much as I hate to say it, I think it's probably time to call it a night, what say you?"

Annie said "no," then took my hand and pulled me toward the door. We entered the living area, but, instead of sitting down or moving to the door, she pulled me in the direction of the bedroom.

On the way, Annie said, "I think it's time I stayed the night. I just want to be with you."

I thought my heart would burst because it was pounding so hard.

Annie said, "I want to shower. Will you join me?"

"Holy shit," I thought.

We then showered, and I got into bed before Annie. She was still doing something in the bathroom.

The full moon shone through the windows giving the room a romantic glow. Annie came out of the bathroom wearing nothing! Her body was highlighted by the moon's glow as she came toward the bed.

I pulled back the covers and she slipped in beside me. We embraced and gently kissed. We were both ready to take it to the next step.

Annie slowly pulled me to her and turned onto her back. Then she pulled me onto her, and I just, naturally, slid between her legs.

We had sex and just lay in each other's arms for a while. It was very satisfying.

I couldn't sleep. My mind went back to the others I had had sex with. I always thought there were only two kinds of girls—those who will and those who won't. Every one of them always said, "Stop," or "No," or "Don't."

After continuing to kiss and I pushed again, one would plea, "please stop," as if they were begging.

Then the third time, they would pull me toward them and we would make love. It's as if they showed me they really wanted to make love but didn't want to appear easy. I just knew I should try again.

The other kind would respond with absolute clarity. When they were pushed the second time, they would say, "I told you no," or "I said stop!" I just knew they meant business. Whether or not we made love, we inevitably ended our relationship soon afterwards.

With Annie, I didn't feel the same. I wanted her more than ever.

We made love for what seemed the whole night long before we finally went to sleep.

Day 7—Seward

I woke up at the sound of Annie softly playing the piano. *"What a way to wake up."*
I got up, put on a robe and went to the piano.

"Good morning sunshine," Annie said.

As I leaned down to kiss her good morning I said, "I think we should live together the last few days of the cruise. I don't think any more harm will be done, and I just want to be with you every minute we have left."

Annie thought for what seemed like forever then smiled and said, "Yes, I think that would be good."

"Let's skip Seward and stay in the penthouse," I told Annie.

"OK," Annie replied.

I then got up, went to the bathroom, relieved myself and brushed my teeth. She then got up from the piano and went to the bathroom.

We then returned to the bed and she kissed me. When she kissed me, I immediately got a tremendous erection.

Annie thought, *"Wow, what an erection."*

Then she climbed onto me and said, "I'll do all the work. Just lie there and enjoy it."

Afterwards, she said, "It's time for some lunch. I need the energy!"

I laughed and said, "OK." We then got dressed and went to the promenade deck.

After lunch, we went back to the penthouse.

Annie said, "I'm going to take a shower."

"Want some company?" I asked.

"No, but you can get undressed," she replied.

I got undressed and was feeling a little self-conscious.

When Annie finished her shower she came out of the bathroom and was completely nude.

Annie went to the piano, played and sang while still nude.

We spent the rest of the afternoon in the penthouse completely nude. It just seemed the natural thing to do.

When it was time to eat, we dressed, and went to dinner. Following dinner, we went to our lounge for the last time.

While we were dancing, I then told Annie that I was going on to Denali State Park for three days and then I had two weeks of leave before I had to report for duty. I asked her, "Will you stay with me until I have to report for duty?" Annie, without any hesitation, said, "Yes, I want to spend as much time together as possible before we have to leave each other." Then we danced until bedtime.

We had one more cocktail before bed and Annie said, "I want to go straight to sleep tonight. I just want you to hold me." I said, "OK," and we both quickly went to sleep in each other's arms.

Denali to San Diego

The next morning, Annie was in her cabin packing and contemplating what she would say to her mother.

Annie thought, *"I have to call Mom and tell her that I'm not coming home, as planned."*

This was the last day of the cruise and Mom would be expecting her home the following day. As she was packing up she began thinking about what she would say to her Mom.

"Wow. This isn't going to be easy," Annie thought as she contemplated the call to her Mom.

She thought about it for a few seconds, *"I'll just have to tell her the truth."*

She dialed the phone.

"Hello," her Mom answered.

Annie said, "Hi Mom, it's me."

"Why haven't you called me?" her Mom asked.

"You told me not to call because you wanted me to think about nothing but the cruise. You said that I should take one day at a time and get away from video games, remote controls, and myself. I did."

Mom replied, "I know I said that, but I didn't think you would actually do it."

Annie then said, "I'm not coming home for another two weeks."

"What? Why?" Mom asked.

She answered, "Well, it's a long story but I met this great guy. He and I fell in love."

Mom was shocked to say the least. Annie had never done anything like this before.

Mom replied, "I don't understand. You'd better tell me all about this guy."

She said, "He's wonderful, handsome and very smart. I want to be with him as long as possible."

Mom asked, "What about school? What about all your plans?"

She replied, "My plans haven't changed."

Mom said, "Now I'm really confused."

Annie explained the situation, and said she would never see him again after this.

"Mom, Jim has only two more weeks of leave left so I'm going to spend it with him in San Diego. We both agreed to go our separate ways at the end of these two weeks. Mom, I just have to do this. I love him and will never see him again."

"Now, I understand," my Mom said, "Enjoy yourself. I'll see you when you get home."

"Thanks for understanding. I love you Mom," and hung up.

Jim and I met for our last breakfast on the ship, and then we returned to our cabins to gather the luggage. Following that we left for the bus ride to Denali.

Annie and I spent the last three days touring Denali National Park. We talked about how to spend our remaining time and we agreed to fly to San Francisco and spend a couple days there.

Then we would rent a car and drive to San Diego after our time in San Francisco.

Believe it or not, we didn't have sex for the next three days.

In San Francisco, we stayed at Fisherman's Wharf, rode trolleys everywhere we could, and toured Chinatown.

We made love in San Francisco for the first time since the penthouse. It was good to feel her close to me again.

The next day, we visited Alcatraz and the Asian Art Museum and took the Segway Electric tour of San Francisco.

We were worn out by the end of the day. We had a late dinner then went straight to bed.

We left San Francisco early in the morning and spent the next night in beautiful Tiburon. There isn't much to see or do in Tiburon but relax. We slept in until 8AM then had the continental breakfast at the hotel.

After breakfast, we spent the rest of the morning walking around the town.

We had lunch and went to Angel Island in the afternoon.

We had an early dinner and went back to the hotel to relax.

We got undressed, and I opened a couple of beers we had bought. We sat and talked for a while.

After a while, I asked, "Do you know your erogenous zones?"

"No, what's that?" she asked.

I explained, "I read, in my medical training, that a body has certain places that excite a person's pleasure zone in the brain. These stimulate the sex drive and ultimately cause an orgasm. It said an orgasm can be achieved with only foreplay."

"I never heard of it," she replied.

"I think we should discover yours," I said.

"Sounds like a plan to me," she said.

I told her, "Actually, the plan is to find the sweet spots and then explore whether the spot should be rubbed, tickled, caressed, or kissed. The spots can be anywhere and are stimulated differently. In order to work properly, you will have to guide me.

First, I find the spot, then you tell me how to best stimulate it in the way that makes the maximum pleasure. Can you do that?"

"I think so," she replied.

"OK. Let's begin with a shower together," I said.

"OK," Annie said, my mind is racing in anticipation of what was going to happen next and thought, "*What am I getting into?*"

We both showered, and then I ran my fingers through her hair, then moving over her face, tracing her lips, ears, and neck.

"My ears and lips are tingling," she said.

I continued working her sweet spots until she had an orgasm.

"This is glorious," she said.

After we finished, we just lay there for a while and then I started gently rubbing her all over. Soon we both fell asleep.

Annie woke the next morning and told me, "This is the best I've ever slept."

I said, "I'm glad. I'm also hungry as a bear awakening from hibernation. Let's eat."

The morning was glorious, and the air had a cool crisp breeze coming off the bay.

We had a very nice breakfast and had a hard time leaving for the road.

Never the less, we drove to Santa Rosa and spent the night in a nice little B & B, sampled wine and just relaxed.

The next day we drove across the state to the gold country on Highway 49. We spent that night in the quaint little town of Sonora.

Then, we drove back across the state to beautiful Carmel. Operating out of Carmel, the first day, we played 18 holes of golf at Pebble Beach. The next day we visited Hearst Castle, and the last day was spent back in Carmel relaxing.

We then drove to Solvang and spent the night. We found a very good German restaurant, ate dinner and then finished with a couple of beers. The next day we went on to Santa Barbara and just relaxed for one night.

We decided to sleep in and then take a leisurely drive to Malibu where we spent two nights. From there we spent two nights in Laguna Beach and then on to Mission Bay, San Diego. Our last three nights were spent on Mission Bay. The last three days were indescribably wonderful. We just relaxed and made a lot of love.

We also talked a lot about our future apart. We both wondered why our commitments should overrule our happiness together. Finally, I said, "Look, we are committed. My next three years will be in SEAL training. When that is finished, I'll call you before I ship out. If, at that time, you are either married or in a relationship we'll just wish each other well and move on. If you aren't, I will know more about the balance of my Navy commitment. Maybe, we can pick up where we left off. For your sake, don't wait for me."

The time seemed to fly by way too fast. The hardest thing I ever did was to say goodbye to Annie. It was especially difficult knowing that we probably would never see each other again.

I took Annie to the airport for her return home. Annie and I kissed and expressed our love for each other, wished each other well, and walked away without looking back.

It was over! I wanted to cry out loud but, somehow, managed to only shed some tears. I wondered, *"Was Annie crying as well?"*

I tried my best to put Annie out of my mind.

Annie Goes Home

‹❦❦❦›

Annie dreaded returning home. *It was going to be a long plane ride to Norfolk,* She thought.

Annie missed Jim already. She wondered how she would put him out of her mind and go on with her life as it was before the cruise. As hard as she tried, Annie just couldn't put Jim out of her mind.

Annie arrived in Norfolk around nine o'clock in the evening. Mom soon pulled up outside the baggage claim area. "Hi Mom, I'm sure glad to be home. I've got so much to tell you that I'm about to burst."

"I take it your vacation went well. I want to know all about this guy, Jim. Did you have fun? Do you have any pictures?" Mom asked.

Annie replied, "Yes I had a wonderful time but no pictures. We decided that we didn't want anything to haunt us. All we have are our memories. I only hope they fade soon."

Mom said, "It's probably a good idea not to have pictures," and followed me to my room.

Annie said, "Oh Mom, the past month was wonderful beyond description. I love him so much I can't believe it. When he looks at me I actually swoon. When he touches me, I tremble all over and I get weak in the knees. He is also thoughtful and considerate.

When we are together, it seems as though he only lives to make me happy.

I miss him terribly already! It hurts so much I can hardly stand it.

I'm never going to see him again. How am I going to deal with this and the hurt?"

Mom hugged me and said, "Well honey, don't say never. You never know what's in the future. You're strong and will handle the future OK. You just have to toughen up and go on."

Annie began to cry as she unpacked and thought about how she could return to her old routine.

"Would I ever be the same?" she wondered.

Maybe we could get together when Jim's commitment is finished. *"Maybe he will be involved with another or, as he said, he might be killed. I have to stop thinking like that."*

That question might have to be answered two weeks later. That's the day Annie missed her menstrual period.

Annie hoped, *"Maybe this is just stress. I'll probably start next month."*

A month later, Annie told her Mom that she had now missed two periods.

Mom said, "Well, I guess you are pregnant. Better go see the doctor."

The doctor confirmed Annie's pregnancy and she lamented, "I've got to find Jim and tell him." Annie made numerous phone calls attempting to find Jim with absolutely no results.

Mom then said, "We should hire a detective agency to find him."

Annie agreed and hired an agency. After about a month, the agency sent her their report. It reported that no such person was in SEAL training at that time. Further, no such person was in the Navy.

"Mom, what am I going to do now?" Annie asked.

Mom said, "We'll just have to make the best of it. Every baby is a blessing, and this one is our blessing. You have to go to Boston as planned and get your PhD. I'll go to Boston, stay with you, and take care of the baby."

Annie said, "Mom, you are such an angel, and I love you so much."

Annie soon gave birth to Robert Randolph. Randolph (Randy) after her step dad.

Annie and her mother stayed in Boston for the next year and a half.

When she received her PhD Annie went to live with her mother to begin her career, as an engineer, in her father's company.

Two years later, Annie married Timothy Baird, and he adopted Randy.

The first year was great. In the second year, Tim began to change. He became verbally abusive, especially to Randy. Their relationship was crumbling and, at the same time, or because of it, Jim Duncan came back into my consciousness. The only way Annie could now make love with Tim was to think about Jim. It was becoming pretty obvious that our marriage was heading over a cliff.

The fact is we were incompatible and never should have married. She doesn't really know why they married. Looking back, Annie knew they were never in love. We were both ports in a storm for each other. That spelled doom from the start and we just didn't see it.

Then one day, Annie had to go away on a week-long business trip. Randy stayed with her mother's while she was gone.

After being gone for only two days, Annie was called back to work because of a business crisis. When she arrived home around 11:30 PM, Annie noticed a car in the driveway that she didn't recognize.

Annie quietly entered the house to keep from waking Tim. She pulled her shoes off and went to the bedroom. Much to her shock, Annie found a woman in bed with Tim. Needless to say, divorce proceedings began immediately. The divorce was amicable, and the adoption was voided by the court.

After the divorce, Annie changed her last name to Jackson and vowed that Tim would be the last man in her life—except for Randy.

This also soured Randy on all men in Annie's life. Randy didn't even want her to date.

SEAL Training

I reported for SEAL "A" School on July 6th.

My mind immediately went into overdrive. I had worked my entire life for this moment and all I could think about was, *"What if I fail?"* I can't think like this.

I thought, *"What about my motto?"*

I repeated it, *"Failure will never overtake me if my determination to succeed is strong enough."*

Then I thought, *"There have been many SEALs before me, and, if they can do it, so can I."*

I didn't know just how many times I would have to repeat these sayings to myself before I was finished, but it was many.

The reality was that becoming a SEAL is an extreme challenge to say the least. I told myself that I was ready for anything they could throw at me.

After passing the Diver/SEAL Physical Screening Test, (PST) I was subjected to the assessment phase.

Because of the extent of my preparation, I easily passed the requirements and was first in every test.

I then entered the 12 week SEAL Training Course at the Naval Special Warfare Preparatory School. A three-week Indoctrination program followed.

Once I passed all the initial screening I attended the 25 weeks Basic Underwater Demolition/SEAL (BUD/S) training at the Naval Special Warfare Center, Naval Amphibious Base Coronado, California.

Following graduation from BUD/S I spent 28 weeks at SEAL Qualification Training including Tactical Air Operations (parachute), Land Warfare, Cold Weather Training and Survival, Evasion, Resistance and Escape (SERE).

After that, I was placed into the pre-indoctrination phase of training known as 'PTRR' (Physical Training Rehabilitation and Remediation).

This is where the real stuff happened. BUD/S was a three-week 'Indoctrination Course', known as INDOC, followed by three phases covering physical conditioning (seven weeks), diving (eight weeks), and land warfare (ten weeks) respectively.

This is well known as "Hell Week". Hell Week was 132 hours of continuous physical activity, which occurred during week three.

Our class lost 79% of our trainees. A student may drop on request (DOR) from the course at any time, by injuries sustained during training or by being cut.

It seemed that I repeated my motto every hour for the entire "Hell Week" . . . and that got me through it.

My final Certification Exercise (CERTEX) was conducted with the entire SEAL Squadron (SQDN) to synchronize Troop (TRP) operations under the Joint Special Operations Task Force (JSOTF) umbrella.

My SEAL training was finally completed on October 1st, 2002, and I was assigned to my first team.

Mission 1 Iraq

My first assignment was as part of the largest single SEAL operation in history from U.S. Naval vessels.

Several days before the beginning of the invasion of Iraq two SEAL Delivery Vehicle (SDV) teams were launched from Mark V Special Operations Craft in the Persian Gulf.

Our objectives were the hydrographic reconnaissance of the Al Basrah (MABOT) and Khawr Al Amaya (KAAOT) Oil Terminals.

I was in one of the SDVs on the way to the oil terminals. I had been training more than three years for this moment, and I don't mind saying the reality of it was beginning to sink in.

I WAS ABOUT TO BE IN COMBAT. Without a doubt I was scared, but, at the same time, I was surprisingly confident and calm. I guess it was the training taking effect.

We had been told that, because of Desert Shield, the Iraqis would strengthen their best troops to defend the oil terminals. These troops were the Royal Guard and were embarrassed in Desert Shield. We were told to expect the fight of our lives.

I think a million thoughts went through my mind including everything they taught in SEAL training.

Then, I remembered my motto, *"Failure will never overtake me if my determination to succeed is strong enough.* Next, I thought, *"Oh shit! Pay attention to your job asshole. You could get your ass shot off."*

The closer we got, the calmer I became. We were nearing the terminals, and I checked all my gear and readied myself for landing and the fight. Then the signal to go was given, and we entered the water.

To our astonishment, there were no Iraqis at all.

After swimming under the terminals and securing our equipment, we spent several hours taking pictures and surveying Iraqi activity on both platforms before returning to our boats.

On 20 March 2003 the Navy SEALs launched what was the largest single SEAL operation in history from U.S. Naval vessels, against the Kuwait Ras al-Qulayah Naval Base and the Ali Al Salem Air Base, as part of a mixed force of U.S. Navy SEALs, Polish GROM, and British Royal Marines.

Our targets were not only the oil platforms but their respective onshore petroleum pumping locks plus the Al Faw port and refinery.

Each force was to be inserted via helicopter or boat on the perimeter of the targets and then assault the main facilities.

The first attacks occurred at the pumping locks for each offshore terminal. At MABOT's pumping lock the team's landing zone was covered in concertina wire that was unreported by their intelligence. As a result, we SEALs and the Royal Marines were forced to hover several feet off the ground.

The Royal Marines were the first off the helicopter followed by us SEALs and all of us immediately became entangled in the obstacles. In this exposed position the SEALs and Marines began taking fire from the platform's garrison.

My adrenaline spiked immediately as we began taking fire from the Iraqis. We returned fire and went on to secure the position. Our actual fighting was minimal, a far cry from what we had expected. None of us could figure out why we just considered ourselves lucky. No one gave it much thought. We were just thankful.

The invasion of Iraq followed and went better and faster than planned.

In just a matter of twenty one days, the initial invasion had ended. I then found myself functioning as a translator for the Marines.

Then next six months was spent in fierce house to house fighting. Following that, my team was sent back to San Diego.

Once I was back in the states, I then had nothing to do but wait for my next assignment. This would become a pattern. I'd wait for weeks or months for a mission. Go through intense mission training. Complete the mission. And once again back to idle time.

The most important thing on my mind was finding Annie.

I checked the phone listings for Mary Ann Harrison. No luck. I then googled her. Again, no luck. I then checked for all Harrisons living in or around Virginia Beach. There were none!

I then hired a detective agency and gave them everything I knew about Annie. That wasn't very much as it turned out.

They completed their search with no results. I had no choice but to assume she married and I stopped looking.

Having been a workaholic and an overachiever all my life, the idle time drove me crazy. I was, for the first time in my life rudderless. I always had the goal of becoming a SEAL. Now that I was a SEAL, I had no goals for myself.

I began to think about what I would do after SEAL duty. I had an engineering degree in computer science, so I wanted a job in my field.

I really had no idea what area of computers I wanted to be involved with, but I knew I should keep up with the latest developments in computers science.

I then spent all my time reading various technical publications.

In order to feed my science fiction addiction, I read Popular Science, Scientific American, and other magazines.

Additionally, I developed the habit of trying to think about how new technology could be applied to improve existing military and fire control systems. I thought this would help prepare me for life after SEALs.

First things first, I couldn't help but wonder what was now in store for me. It was now September and all of a sudden it dawned on me that winter was not far away. I thought, *"Oh shit! It could become very uncomfortable soon."*

With any luck, my next assignment would require training that would keep me in San Diego through the winter. Now, I couldn't think about anything but what was in store for me next. The idle time got so bad that I anxiously wanted to receive my next assignment soon. At least then, the suspense would be over. Ten days later I was called to pick up my orders.

I was filled with trepidation. I, somehow, knew my life was about to change forever. I figured it was either back to Iraq or go to Afghanistan. Neither sounded good.

The CIA

⁓⁓⁓

S ure enough, my new assignment was the one that would define my life, not only while I was a SEAL, but for my entire career. This assignment was with Special Forces. I was told I would be going to Saudi Arabia. I thought, *"How can they always do something that you never figured on?"*

In September, 2003, I was entered into a total immersion language school for increasing my Arabic proficiency. I also received my Saudi identity. I would become Abdul Mujahid Rahid. I was also ordered to stop shaving.

After my basic language training, I was sent to a secret training unit outside Riyadh, Saudi Arabia. There I was trained in Afghan Pashto language and culture. They had built an entire Afghan village complete with Afghan residents. The idea was to exactly replicate life in Afghanistan. We were all supposed to be Afghan refugees that fled Afghanistan seeking asylum in Saudi Arabia. Some actually were refugees brought out by the CIA.

After six weeks of being taught Pashto, I was given a job as a Saudi courier working for the American Embassy. I spent the next six months learning Riyadh streets, landmarks, and even small details.

One day, my unit commander called me to his office. He said, "We have an assignment we would like you to consider. It's beyond the regular kind of assignment and, as such, it is volunteer only.

Our intelligence tells us that there is a major Al-Qaeda cell in an area close to Alishang, Afghanistan. There is an anti-Taliban group also operating there. We believe that in order to penetrate both groups, we will have to have two agents act as a local married couple. We need you to work with a female agent in Afghanistan. You would be set up with a cover story to explain your presence there as a Saudi married to an Afghan.

The female agent we selected is an Afghan with an American father and an Afghan mother. She went to the United States when she was five years old. She attended school and attended college in the USA. She was recruited by the CIA after graduating college and sent back to Afghanistan.

We believe she is perfect for this assignment, but women in Afghanistan simply cannot operate without a husband.

The Afghan culture prohibits women from socializing outside the home. This makes it essential that you both are sufficiently compatible to last long enough to complete the assignment. The assignment will have you living as a couple for up to five years in Afghanistan.

Your task would be to connect with married men and then, somehow, get involved as couples. In that way, your Afghan wife could possibly gather intelligence through the wives.

I have to tell you that it will be both difficult and dangerous.

Can you see yourself accepting such an assignment?" Before you answer, I want you to know that if you decline the assignment, you will be sent to Afghanistan as a translator and no questions will be asked. In either case, you are going to Afghanistan. I don't think that's any surprise.

I replied, "Yes sir, it's no surprise, and I accept the assignment as requested." The commander then said, "Good. As I already said, your assignment will be difficult in many ways but one particular difficulty is to ensure the two of you are sufficiently compatible to successfully carry out this mission.

Toward that end, we have devised a test for the both of you. The test lasts 72 hours and consists of two parts.

Part one is like marriage counseling.

The two of you will be put into a small hotel room where you will spend 24 hours together.

You will sleep in the same bed, but there will be a long body pillow between you.

You are not to have any physical contact during the entire 24 hour period.

Cameras and microphones will monitor everything you do or say.

There is no music, TV, or radios. There is a telephone in the room but it only goes to the psychiatrist. You can only call him if you want to withdraw from the test. You can withdraw for any reason.

Each of you will be given a list of 100 questions or topics. There is a scale that goes from 1 to five in two directions. The "Up" scale indicates like and the "Down" scale indicates dislike.

You are not to disclose your grading to each other. You both are to record the degree you like or dislike the topic. You can discuss anything but the scores. The idea is to get to know each other well enough to believe you can co-exist. You have all day to decide.

The next morning the psychiatrist will bring your breakfast and take your graded questions. While you are eating breakfast, he will evaluate your grades for compatibility.

At that time, a decision will be made by both of you as to whether or not you will proceed with the assignment as a couple.

Then, the psychiatrist, at his sole discretion, will determine whether the two of you are compatible enough to continue. If you are considered compatible, the test will continue. If you are determined to be in-compatible, the test will be terminated and you both will be reassigned to regular duty."

If you are deemed acceptable, you will proceed to part two where you will spend another 48 hours in the same room. All cameras and microphones will be removed and the two of you will do whatever you want and discuss anything except your real selves.

Again, either of you can terminate the test, for any reason, and no questions will be asked.

"Any questions?"

"No sir,"

"Do you accept the assignment?" he asked.

"Yes sir,"

"Then here's the plan. Your Afghan wife is an American operating under an alias. She went to the United States when she was seven years old where she was educated. Upon graduation from college, she was recruited into the CIA, and then assigned to Afghanistan in 2003 as a translator. She is to be your Afghani wife named Ara Marwat Rahid.

Neither of you will know anything about each other's real history. You will each learn everything about your CIA created histories.

You will continue to use James Duncan as your American alias and Abdul Rahid as your Arabic name.

Your cover story is that you are the son of a very wealthy Saudi that financially supports you. You were educated in England where you met your wife. After college, your wife returned to Afghanistan, so you decided to marry her and live in Afghanistan. You will be thoroughly trained in your new roles.

That will be all for now. You are to report here at 0700 and bring nothing. Everything you need will be supplied to you for the test period."

I left for my room with my mind racing.

I thought, *"What a turn of events. I wouldn't, in a million years, have imagined such an assignment. Shit, now I will be in Afghanistan in the winter but I would also have a wife! Wow!"*

I went to bed but just lay there in anticipation for a very long time before I fell asleep.

My New Wife

I got up, dressed and arrived at the commander's office at 0700 hours.

There was a woman wearing a full burka waiting, and I assumed she was my partner. It's impossible to determine whether she is pretty or ugly because her burka covered her completely.

She looked in my direction, and I felt as though she was trying to look deep into my soul.

I sat down next to her so those eyes couldn't look directly at me.

Neither of us spoke a word. A couple of minutes later, we were called into the commander's office and introduced to a psychiatrist and to each other.

The psychiatrist then began to talk, "I will lay out the rules for the first 48 hour part. First, I want to be specific about what the conditions are," he said.

"They are:

1. You must not dislike each other.
2. You must learn each other's cover history.

In case one of you is ever suspected and interrogated, you must know each other like only a wife or husband would know. Toward that end, you will spend the last 48 hours in the hotel room completely nude.

The cameras and microphones will be removed. The door has been removed from the bathroom and only very small towels will be issued. The idea is to prevent either of you from hiding any part of you. You will even have to see, smell, and hear, each other fart, urinate, and defecate.

You will begin part two by examining each other's body visually as if you were conducting an autopsy.

First, you will each shower. Then, Abdul, you will visually examine Ara first. You will then identify all anomalies such as blemishes, moles, warts, tattoos, body tags and/or birthmarks. You will determine whether her breasts are the same size or not, whether or not one breast is higher or lower than the other, then the physical contours of the body.

Ara, you will then visually examine Abdul in the same manner as he did.

When both visual examinations are completed, Abdul will perform the blindfold examination.

Abdul, you will start your examination by feeling the head to determine any bumps or irregularities.

Your hands and fingers will then feel every inch of her body, including whether or not she has hemorrhoids.

You are to determine if Ara has any warts on the lips of her vagina not visible.

Ara, you will then examine Abdul by touch the same way including whether the penis is circumcised or not, note the size, length, width, and which testicle hangs lower than the other as well as his toes and fingers.

Is everything clearly understood?"

"Yes," we both said.

"Now, both of you must state your agreement to continue or withdraw."

Abdul said, "I agree to continue."

Ara said, "I agree to continue."

Now, the psychiatrist said, "Ara, take off your burka."

For the first time, I saw her. I would classify Ara as good looking but not beautiful. I still had no idea what kind of personality she had.

The psychiatrist asked, "Do either of you have any questions before you are sequestered?"

Both replied, "No."

The psychiatrist added, "There is one last thing. We believe including sex in your relationship actually provides more credibility of your being married. We would prefer that your relationship included sex but it is optional."

With that said, we were both driven to the hotel and locked in. We were told to go inside, completely disrobe, and put our clothing into a large trash bag they had been given.

We both undressed and put our clothes bag outside the door.

Well, there we were, stark naked giving each other the once over.

I then suggested, "Shall we shower before we examine each other."

"OK. Shall we shower together?

I said "Yes, might as well. We showered together and I asked, "Are you ready to get started?"

"Yes, let's get going," Ara replied.

There was a scale in the bathroom and we each weighed ourselves.

I stepped on the scale and Ara said, "195 pounds."

She looked at me and said, "I see you have no body fat. My God, you're just bones and muscle.

Well, I can't make out any defining facial features through your beard. Is there anything under there that I should know about? Any dimples, scars, moles, or other blemishes?"

"No. I'm as smooth as a baby's ass." I said.

"I see you have a small tattoo. Who is ANNIE?"

"She was my first love but we are history now," I replied.

"What happened?"

"It's a long story. For now, just say that we broke up," I said.

"Well, other than being a walking skeleton, you look pretty good." she said.

Ara thought, *"I believe I can live with him."*

"OK, it's time for my visual examination of you." I said.

Ara was 5'6" tall and weighed 130lbs. She had dark hair, brown eyes and looked pure Afghani. Her body had absolutely no blemishes or distinguishing marks except for a small dark birthmark inside her right knee. Everything else was exactly where it was supposed to be. Ara had a near perfect body.

I completed my visual examination and said, "OK. It's your turn to do the blindfold examination of me.

I thought, *"For sure, we'll find out whether or not we can tolerate or like each other after this examination."*

Ara then, as requested, put on her blindfold and began.

When her blindfolded examination of me had gotten to my genitals, she found that I had a massive erection. She felt my penis and balls and said, "I think you're voting that we should include sex in our relationship. Is that correct?"

I replied, "Sure."

"Well, this is my vote and she slowly stood up. When she was standing up, she kissed me."

Ara finished her visual examination and I said, "I think it's time to go to bed. I'm having a hard time keeping my hands off you. You know, we did vote."

Ara replied, "I thought you would never ask."

We then finished the examinations with a very good sexual encounter. Everything went surprisingly well, and we found that we might actually like each other. Additionally, we seem to have quite a lot in common.

Ara was, apparently, well-educated, but I couldn't figure out what she majored in.

She seemed very likeable but I could sense that she had a cold blooded side typical of CIA field agents.

I thought back to those piercing eyes behind the burka.

She seemed highly intelligent and unflappable.

We completed the examination phase, and were approved for the assignment. We then immediately left for Kabul.

After arriving in Kabul, we went to our orientation meeting. When we got there, we were greeted by, none other than my old friend from my high school days Commander Al Smith. It was great seeing him again.

Al said we would be working for him and that the CIA had developed an actual class to teach us about our characters and how to live the lifestyle the CIA thought would best serve the mission's purpose.

After our orientation meeting, Al took us to dinner. We talked about how he wanted to operate and communicate. Al stressed, "No one should ever know you are in the CIA or military."

Because Ara is Afghani, she would be the only go-between with any American if you ever feel the need to connect anyone to us. The only contact on our side will be me, and I am only supposed to be a casual acquaintance. My job will be an American working as an administrator in the U.S. Embassy.

Once a connection is made with anyone, I will take it from there. I will then decide whether or not the relationship goes further.

After dinner, Ara and I went to our room.

I went to the refrigerator and got us a beer. As I did, I said, "Well, what do you think now?"

"I don't know what to think. I'm still confused. I guess we will understand more tomorrow."

I replied, "Yes, I guess so."

"What is Commander Smith like?"

"He's a great guy. Smart and a no bullshit kind of guy. You always know where you stand."

"How long have you known him?"

"I've known him since I was in high school. I joined the San Diego Iron Man Club, and he was a member there."

"So you trust him?"

"With my life", I replied.

We just sat and talked about where all this might lead. Ara seemed to have something on her mind so I didn't say anything.

Finally, she said, "Something is bothering me, so I'd better get it off my chest. I hope you can forgive me."

I asked, "Why do you say that?"

Then she said, "I haven't been completely honest. I withheld something important." She expressed her concern that I might find her difficult to live with.

Ara said, "I'm very stubborn by nature and I'm very outspoken. I should have told you and the psychiatrist."

I replied, "I'm sure that won't be a problem."

"Why?" she asked.

"Because I'm such a nice guy," I said and laughed.

She looked at me with a serious look on her face and said, "I'm serious you jackass."

I laughed again and replied, "I'm serious, too. I really am a nice guy but more importantly, I'm very easy going; in fact, I would much rather you are straight forward and honest in expressing your thoughts and feelings. The job we have to do together would get us both killed if we aren't absolutely honest and uninhibited in our relationship. Trust between us is everything."

Ara said, "Now I feel better. We are going to be just fine."

"Good. Let's go to bed. I'm tired. I need to get a good night's sleep before starting our training and life as a married couple."

Training

The next morning we got dressed and went to our classroom. The class opened with us each being given a large envelope.

In the envelope I received were identifications, a bank account statement showing $100,000 in it, credit/debit cards, and a thick manuscript. The manuscript described, in minute detail, everything about our roles and cover stories. We were told that our objectives were very simple. They were:

1. Meet people
2. Create as many close relationships as possible
3. Gather intelligence

In order to accomplish our mission, we were to be a free spending, party going couple.

We knew this would be controversial but, ultimately, work in our favor by attracting only the kind of people we wanted.

Our intent, generally, was, that I would meet men and tell them that I was trying to find a brother, Mohammed, that was supposed to be somewhere in the area but I didn't know where.

My story was that my brother had come to Pakistan with a group of Saudi friends led by a Saudi named Osama Bin Laden. I had heard that they left Afghanistan and were somewhere in Northwestern Pakistan. My plan was to find my brother and join his group.

As for the training itself, Ara and I were separated into different rooms for the first week. Here, we were given the details of our fictitious history. The reason we were separated is that each of us was to learn our individual histories in detail so, theoretically, we couldn't remember small details of the other's history. This would provide some degree of credibility if ever interrogated. This briefing was repeated every day for a week.

The second week consisted of us being interrogated by CIA agents in an attempt to catch us making mistakes. This process reinforced our learning every detail. By the time it was completed, we were psychologically and emotionally into our new characters. i.e., we actually were reborn.

The third and fourth weeks were spent jointly learning the names of key people, contacts, the area and the latest intelligence.

We completed the intense training and left for our new adventure. From now on, we would be Abdul and Ara Rahid and live in Alishang, Afghanistan.

Alishang, Afghanistan

⚜

Ara and I were transferred to the CIA Office in Jalalabad, Afghanistan in late August, 2005 and reported exclusively to Commander Al Smith.

Our orders were to move into an upscale housing compound in Alishang, Afghanistan.

This type of home is typical of the wealthy. The building had been built by the CIA complete with a secret room that contained a powerful computer and satellite communications.

It was built on a large piece of land surrounded by a high mud wall. Inside the walls were two large housing units and two smaller ones. One smaller unit was used as a guest house and the other was for live-in caretakers. There was also a large six car garage.

A very large garden area was in the center of the compound. As you entered, there was a large water fountain. Beyond that was a greenhouse about 40 feet by 40 feet. It was constructed over a six foot hole in the ground. At ground level was a wall to wall wooden deck. Under the deck were electric generators and water pumps that supplied the whole compound. In one corner of the greenhouse was a large Jacuzzi. The greenhouse had ceiling heaters so it could be used in winter. Lounge chairs were scattered around the deck. This type of compound was very unusual for Afghanistan, especially in a small town like Alishang. The compound was completely self-contained. The second main house was completely furnished but unused.

The CIA had caretakers already moved in. This family was supposed to be a man, his wife and two sons in their early twenties; in fact, they were all CIA operatives. The man and woman actually were caretakers, but the two sons were our guards. It was a very nice set up.

Another ruse was that we were looking for a family to rent the empty house. That gave us the opportunity to regularly bring CIA operatives into the compound without suspicion.

What a place to live. On the first floor was a large kitchen open to a large living area. It was very nice for entertaining in the American way. It had a formal dining room and a Hujra (Men's room). It also had a built-in bar that opened to both the living area and the Hujra. It had two large bathrooms, one private and the other for guests.

Upstairs was a large bedroom, bath, big walk-in closets, and another room we used as a den. Secretly wedged between the walk-in closets was a secret communications room.

Last, but not least, we had two British Land Rover Defender, seven passenger, station wagons. The Land Rovers were equipped for off-road operation, satellite GPS and communications. It also had some armor plating and one-way tinted windows that allowed passengers to see out but could not be seen from the outside. One Rover was for the caretakers and one for me. We settled in as fast as we could. Actually, we appeared almost like any Afghan couple except we were wealthy.

I just didn't like this country. It is made up of tribal regions and operated under their own rules regardless of the law. The country simply sucks. On the other hand, it's not even a real country. There are no jobs here as we know jobs. Afghanistan offers few ways for a man to support his family: join the opium trade, farm, raise sheep, or join the army. That's about it. Those are the options.

Oh, I forgot, you can also live in a refugee camp and eat plum-sweetened, crushed beetle paste and squirt mud like a goose with stomach flu, if that's your idea of living.

The smell alone of those 'tent cities of the walking dead' is enough to hurl you into the poppy fields to cheerfully scrape bulbs for eighteen hours a day.

To our mutual relief, Ara and I liked each other. It's a good thing because we will have to live like this for a long time.

Since marriages in Afghanistan were typically arranged or forced, we appeared to be authentic.

Except for the wealthy aristocracy, life in Afghanistan was very hard. In remote villages like Alishang, there was nothing to do but survive from day to day.

We've been living with these Tajiks, Uzbeks, Turkmen and even a couple of Pashtuns, for over a month-and-a-half now. This much I can say for sure—these guys, all of them, are barbarians . . . actual, living barbarians.

They live to fight. It's what they do. It's all they do. They have no respect for anything, not for their families, not for each other, not for themselves. They claw at one another as a way of life.

They play polo with a goat carcass and force their five-year-old sons into human cockfights to defend the family honor. They are barbarians, roaming packs of savage, heartless beasts who feed on each other's barbarism. They are simply cavemen with AK-47's.

This country blows my mind. There are no roads, there's no infrastructure, and there is no effective national government.

This is just an inhospitable, rock pit shit hole ruled by eleventh century warring tribes. There is no recreation other than coffee shops and socializing Afghan style. The men socialize together and the women socialize together. They don't socialize in mixed company. This lifestyle either makes couples hate each other or, develops affection between them. I think, maybe, love doesn't exist except between mother and child.

Oh well, enough about this shit hole. In our case, it actually worked to create affection between Ara and me. I think that's because we had a purpose bigger than we are. Our purpose was to gather intelligence. It's all about intelligence. Another way it helped us was that we hoped we would become a great place to go. That made us much wanted friends to have.

Making friends was a very difficult thing to do. I tried my best to meet men but being a Saudi I was viewed with suspicion. The only thing I could do was keep trying and hope the ice would break soon.

As luck would have it, one day two guys came into a café and sat next to me. I overheard them talking and recognized a Saudi accent. I decided to chance speaking in Arabic. I said, "Pardon me but I couldn't help hearing your accent. Are you Saudi?"

The man replied, in Arabic, "Yes, are you?"

I answered, "I'm from Riyadh. My name is Abdul."

The Saudi replied, "My name is Mohammed and my friend's name is Assad. He is from Alishang. Please join our table."

I signaled the waiter and had my food moved to their table. We sat there for more than an hour.

Mohammed then said, "My friend, we must leave you now. It's been nice talking to you."

I replied, "Maybe you would like to come to my house sometime and we can enjoy some Saudi food and share more conversation."

Mohammed said, "That would be good. When?"

I said, "What about Friday night around five o'clock?"

We agreed and they left.

I thought, *"Maybe the ice is finally broken."*

Both Mohammed and Assad came as agreed and we spent the evening having dinner followed by drinks. Before leaving, Mohammed said, "I'm sorry I don't have a home to invite you to, but I would like to take you to dinner before I leave Alishang."

"I'd like that, thank you," I said. We set the time and they left.

We met at a little restaurant that I hadn't known about.

Assad said, "The place isn't much, but I like it and come here often."

During dinner, Mohammed told me that he lived in Pakistan and only visited Alishang occasionally.

"This could be a big break. Maybe he was an insurgent."

I decided to chance telling them, "I have a brother somewhere in Pakistan. Would you by any change know him? His name is Mohammed Rahid?"

"Sorry, no," Mohammed said, "Do you know where he lives?"

I said, "No, he came here a few years ago and the last I heard from him was that he was going to Pakistan near the Afghan border. I've been looking for him."

Mohammed then said, "I'll ask around when I get back home and let you know if I find out anything. If I locate him, I'll tell him where you are."

I said, "Thank you very much. I appreciate your kindness."

When it was time to go, I invited Assad back to our house and he readily accepted.

With this contact, I began meeting men and developing relationships. Mohammed and some of his friends became regulars, and my contact expansion was under way.

It turned out that the restaurant where I met Mohammed and Assad was a Taliban gathering place. I became a regular there and known by the owners and their regulars. In other words, my credentials were becoming established.

Ara and I discussed ways to expand our contacts to include spouses.

We were feeling pretty good about our progress to date when I was called to Jalalabad to meet with Al Smith.

Mission 2, JTAC

One day in August, 2005 I was temporarily attached to a Marine unit in support of the Afghan government forces. My job was to help direct heavy American aerial bombardment of Taliban positions within the mountain fortress.

I was to locate Al-Qaeda strongholds then act as a JTAC (Joint Terminal Attach Controller) for A10 Warthog aircraft.

I would talk the A10 pilots to the targets then stay there long enough to assess the damage. If everything targeted did not get taken out, I would have to redirect them until the raid was successful.

Sometimes, this got very dangerous. The bad guys were very good at finding us JTACs. They had a very high priority on killing us. This also got to be routine which is very hazardous. It made some guys careless which resulted in their capture or death.

I dropped by chopper in a remote area to infiltrate behind Taliban lines. I was all alone, a one man show.

I was now deep in enemy territory and insurgents were all around me.

I wondered, *"What the hell am I doing in this God forsaken place? This could get a guy killed—dead."*

Then, I thought about my motto. If I ever needed it, now was the time.

My first action in Iraq was a walk in the park compared to this.

In Iraq, I had an entire army around me but now I'm alone. I must confess that I'm scared as hell.

But, *"Hey, I got to do what I got to do."*

With my heart in my throat, I inched my way to the target area. When I got into position, I called in the Warthogs.

After the strike, the Warthogs stayed around to give me and the rescue chopper cover.

I can tell you that that chopper was the most beautiful thing I had ever seen except for Annie.

"Thank you Og Mandino,"

I would later be awarded the Silver Star for this action.

Back in Alishang

On my way back from the mission, I stopped in Jalalabad for mission debriefing.

After debriefing Al said, "Intelligence given me indicates there is a woman named Begom Jan Ahmad living in Alishang that may be anti-Taliban. Your job is to make contact with her and check out her sympathies."

Al gave me her last known address, and I left for Alishang.

On the way home, my mind went back to Ara. I wondered how she was doing and what she might have accomplished while I was away.

I had been gone only a few days, but I missed her. I was surprised how much I looked forward to holding her and just talking to her.

I got home around 1630 and quietly opened the door. Ara was in the kitchen.

I sneaked in and said, "Anybody got anything a man could eat around this dump?"

Ara turned, screamed, and ran into my arms.

"God, it's good to see you", I said.

Ara replied, "It's good to see you too. I'll fix something special if you can wait. I want to celebrate."

"Sounds wonderful. I feel like celebrating too."

I took a shower, pulled on some sweats, and poured us Jack Daniels on the rocks.

I stood in the kitchen while Ara cooked. She told me that she had not done much since I left so she decided to just relax while I was gone.

"I'm glad you are rested because I plan to wear us both to a frazzle."

Ara replied, "Promises, promises" and laughed.

I said, "Just wait and I'll show you promises."

After dinner, I fulfilled the promise and then slept like a baby all night.

I woke up the next morning and felt extraordinarily happy. Ara and I just relaxed for the next couple of days. Then I went back to the restaurant. It was old home week.

"Abdul, where the hell you been?" the owner asked.

"I heard a rumor that my brother was down south near Kandahar so I went there looking for him. Much to my disappointment it was just a baseless rumor."

"Sorry", he replied.

I met a couple of new guys and invited them to dinner. They both said yes. Then, Ara and I quickly got back into our routine.

Ara and I discussed how we could meet this Begom Jan Ahmad. Ara suggested we simply knock on her door and say we heard she may be looking for a home to rent. Then, we just keep a conversation going long enough to be invited into her house. If successful in getting inside, we can invite her over for dinner.

We then went to the address given to us and knocked on the door. A big, but well built, woman answered the door and said, "May I help you?"

Ara replied, "A thousand pardons. My name is Ara Rahid and this is my husband, Abdul. We have been led to believe you might be looking for a home to rent and we have a beautiful house in our complex that you might like."

Begom Jan looked puzzled and said, "Sorry, I'm not."

Ara quickly replied, "Sorry we bothered you. Could we talk to you for a few minutes if you're not too busy? We are new here in Alishang and would like to ask you a few questions."

Begom Jan hesitated for a few seconds then said, "Sure, won't you come in?"

Ara said, "Thank you so much."

We entered the house and quickly saw it was very tiny and poorly furnished. I thought, "*What a way to live. At least it is very clean.*"

Begom Jan offered us tea and we gladly accepted.

We sat down and Ara began, "First, we recently moved here and don't know anyone. We are hoping to find someone to rent the vacant house. Since we were obviously misinformed, let me apologize for coming to see you unannounced."

"That's quite all right" Begom Jan said.

Then I said, "Maybe you know of our complex?"

I gave her the address and said, "Is there a doctor near there that you would recommend?"

Begom Jan said, "I know where it is but I'm sorry I don't know anyone near there. I'll ask some of my friends if you like."

I wrote down our phone number and said, "Thank you so much. I appreciate any help you can give us."

Ara continued asking about places to shop and just chit chatting. Begom Jan seemed to enjoy talking to Ara.

Actually, Begom Jan was very friendly and gracious. She and Ara talked for almost an hour.

I interrupted saying, "Ara, I think we've taken up enough of this good lady's time. Then I turned to Begom Jan and said, "Thank you for your kind hospitality."

Ara said, "Oh my. Yes, we must go. Thank you for your hospitality."

Begom Jan replied, "It was a pleasure meeting you. I enjoyed our visit."

Ara said, "Would we be out of line if Abdul and I invited you to our home for dinner?"

Begom Jan responded, "Not at all if it includes my husband, Ali."

Ara said, "Of course, your husband as well. Is Friday night OK?"
She replied, "Yes, that would be fine."

We left feeling very elated that our guise worked so well.

Friday came and the Ahmads came. We had dinner and talked to past midnight. We all seemed to hit it off and agreed to have them over again.

It seemed our house was always full of people. Between our socializing, and CIA operatives coming and going, the entire compound was always a beehive of activity.

In order to avoid suspicion, we told all our guests that we lived in one house, a large family lived in another, and the compound caretakers with their two sons lived in the other house. One house was vacant, and we were looking for someone to rent it.

After Ara and I became convinced that our friendships with the some of the locals were good enough, we chanced probing into their religious and political views.

Most couples didn't have strong views one way or the other. Our new friends, Ali and Begom Jan Ahmad, seemed different.

One night we decided it was time to tell them that we were both college educated. This was something Afghanis tended to keep secret. Afghans, generally, were very afraid to expose themselves or their opinions to anyone but trusted friends of like minds.

Our openness seemed to break down a barrier. Once they decided we were to be trusted, they eagerly confessed that they were also educated. After a couple of weeks, we decided the time had come to test them further.

One night Ara casually commented, "I think it's a disgrace the way women are denied an advance education," Begom Jan instantly and emphatically replied, "Yes."

This was just the kind of opening we had hoped for. From that moment on, all barriers began coming down. Before long, we were openly and frankly talking politics. Ali and Begom Jan were very much anti-Taliban.

One night, Begom Jan swore us to secrecy. Then she said, "First I must tell you about me and why I am dedicated to an organization named Human Equal Rights (HER).

I had a bad life until I was fifteen years old. This experience caused me to become an activist in human rights. First, I want to tell you my story.

I was born a Hazara, in a little village north of Ghazni. We were poor and my father, Faiz, was a very cruel brute. He was a very large man, six feet five inches and weighed 260 lbs.

My mother, Adila, was five feet one inch and weighed 120 lbs. My father regularly beat me and my mother.

I was very defiant beginning as far back as I can remember. I would do things to antagonize him and would always be beaten until the blood flowed. My mother would try to intervene and would also be beaten.

My father would tell me something, and I would intentionally say I didn't hear him.

Once, he was so infuriated that he cut off part of my right ear and said, 'I'll teach you about an eye for an eye, you bitch. Maybe now you will hear me.'

This kind of treatment went on as long as I lived in his house.

I was always very big for my age and big for being a girl. By the time I was eleven, I was as tall as my mother. Additionally, I began puberty during my tenth year. My pubic hair appeared, and I began developing breasts.

I attended school until I finished the sixth grade. When I turned twelve, I was five feet four inches and had a fully developed body.

The day after school was out my father called me to the living room and said, "your school is over but your education is not. You will soon be old enough for marriage, and I will now teach you how to be a proper wife.

A wife's only responsibilities are to please your husband, bear him sons, and keep his house. You already know how to keep a house so I will teach you how to be a wife. Now, it is time to see how your body has developed. Take off all your clothes and stand before me."

I looked quizzically at my mother and she said, 'You must do as your father says.'

Then, I removed all my clothes except my underwear.

'All of them,' he bellowed. I then, reluctantly, took everything off.

'Come close to me,' he ordered.

He then looked me over and said, 'Turn around slowly.'

After I turned completely and facing him again, he said, 'Spread your feet apart.'

He then said, 'You look ready for your lessons to begin.'

Next, he pulled off his pants and pulled me close to him.

He said, 'Take my dick in your hands.

You have to learn how to handle a dick properly.' He then took my hand and made my fingers wrap around his dick and slowly jacked him off.

It was very embarrassing for me.

This was done every day for the next week after dinner was finished and the kitchen was cleaned.

A week later, my father said, 'It's time for your next lesson.

You are to give me oral sex.

First, your mother will show you how to do it properly.

Then tomorrow, you will begin your lesson.'

My mother then gave him oral sex, and he told me how to make it feel the best for him.

I then, for the next week, gave him oral sex every night in the living room.

The problem was that I would not put my lips on his penis. In effect, I would put his dick in my mouth but I didn't give him real oral sex at all. This infuriated him, but I would never do it correctly. He would slap or hit me, curse, and push me away. He finally gave up on oral sex.

Now came my next lesson, except it was done in the bedroom where he raped me. I resisted and would simply lay still. This infuriated him. He would say, "You will be a worthless wife.

I then became his sex partner until I was thirteen.

On my thirteenth birthday, my father said, 'I have found you a husband, and you will be married tomorrow.'

I couldn't question him because this was the custom. Besides, I thought I was getting out of my father's house. My husband's house couldn't be any worse. Actually, I was excited about the prospect of marriage. I would have a home and husband who would take care of me.

I figured that if I took good care of his house and was respectful to him, he might even like me.

We were married the next day.

His name was Gholam Ahktar Mohammed and he was thirty three years old.

On our wedding night, he literally raped me. He was completely insensitive and inconsiderate. He was exactly like my father. I was simply the new property he had bought.

Well, so much for my earlier thoughts and hopes. My life with him was exactly the same as in my father's house. Life went on this way for the next two years.

Our houses had a wooded area behind them that stretched most of the way around the village. My father's house was not far from my house, and I regularly sneaked to visit with my mother. My father had forbidden me to come to his house or see my mother. One day, while I was visiting mother, my father unexpectedly came home. He was furious.

He said, 'You have disobeyed me again. You have disgraced my house again.'

He then hit me, grabbed me by the hand, and pulled me to the door.

'I'll take you to your husband and tell him he has to punish you.'

He began to walk through the woods very fast making it hard for me to keep up with him.

I was more mad than frightened and began to resist.

He then yanked so hard it made me fall.

Then, he took my left arm in both his hands and pulled me to my feet.

As he did so, both his arms raised over his head exposing the dagger he always carried.

When I was on my feet, without thinking, I grabbed the dagger and thrust it into his belly.

He bent down, looked shocked, and then looked up at me with surprise on his face.

When he did, I simply slit his throat.

I kept his dagger and quietly walked back to my house.

It was weeks before they found his body.

One day, someone came to my house to tell me that my father had been killed.

Apparently, I was never suspected, and I never heard any more about it.

Then my husband's brother, Katib and his wife, Bibi Gul, came here to visit his mother Lakhta.

Katib was different. He was the first man I ever met who was kind and considerate. He had been educated in the USA and now worked for the Americans. I didn't know men like him existed.

I would regularly go to the market alone to get fresh vegetables and meat for dinner. Women were not supposed to go out without a family male, but I frequently had to go because my husband worked and I had to have his dinner when he came home. Well, this day was different.

As I walked to the market, I saw three Taliban soldiers approaching me. I was now very frightened.

When they got to me they asked, 'Where is your escort?'

Before I could say anything one of them said, 'Why don't we have some fun?'

With that, they dragged me between two buildings and each of them raped me. After raping me, they beat me bloody and said, 'This should teach you to disobey rules,' and they laughed. I was nearly unconscious and left there to die.

When I didn't return home, my aunt came looking for me. She found me and took me back home where she cleaned and bound my wounds.

When my husband came home, he went into a rage and cursed me every other word. He called me a whore. He said, 'It's your fault! You shouldn't have gone out alone. You have disgraced my house.' He then grabbed me and began beating me. 'You don't deserve to live. I'll have you stoned,' he threatened.

Knowing he would have Begom Jan killed, Katib said, 'Please, Gholam, can I buy her?'

He paused and asked, 'Why would you want her?'

Katib said, 'I need a housekeeper and I like her.'

'How much will you give?' he asked.

'One hundred dollars,' he answered.

'Only because you are my brother will I do this,' he said.

Katib paid him and took me to Kabul.

As we were going to Kabul, Katib and Bibi Gul confessed that they couldn't keep me.

However, Bibi Gul said, 'I have a friend that you might be able to live with as a housekeeper.

I will ask him when we get home.'

After arriving in Kabul, Bibi Gul called her friend, Ajmal Khan Alizai, and told him the story.

He quickly agreed to hire me as a housemaid and Nanny to his daughter.

I moved into his house and met the household staff.

After meeting the staff, he introduced me to his daughter Maryam who was four years younger than me.

From that moment on, Maryam and I became like sisters.

Maryam's father said, 'you will also attend school with Maryam. She will help you with your studies.'

He then told Maryam, 'When you help Begom Jan, you will master your own studies and learn to teach and communicate better. Maryam loved teaching me. It built her self-esteem and confidence.

Mister Alizai was a very kind man and fervently believed in equal rights for women.

He taught Maryam and me that we could do anything if we put our minds to it. His encouragement was never ending. He was, truly, a great human being, and I loved him like a father.

I was extremely fortunate, and I will forever be grateful to my aunt, uncle, and Mister Alizai. That is why I do what I do."

Ara said, "Wow, what a story. I'm very sorry."

Begom Jan then told me that she would like me to join HER. Of course I said yes. She then told me all about the organization and its struggles to get women involved. She told me that her friend, Maryam, was the head of HER.

"Abdul and I are very happy to be a part of HER," I told Begom Jan.

We felt this could be very useful in the future. We continued to invest our time with the locals.

I reported our situation to Al Smith and that we were sure they were to be trusted.

Al agreed and said. "Take the relationship wherever it leads and let me know when, or if, you think I should enter the picture."

On our intelligence gathering mission, we have one basic factor working in our favor. That factor is truth. The Taliban cannot escape the fact, believe it or not, they are still human beings.

That means they have to eat food and drink water. That requires couriers and that comes in very handy. We track the couriers, locate the tunnel entrances and storage facilities, type the info into our handhelds, and shoot the coordinates to the satellite link connected to the Highers.

The other part of our job is to form relationships with sympathetic locals to give us more eyes and ears.

I continued to spend much of my time in coffee shops trying to get acquainted with as many locals as possible. I soon developed friendships with two local men.

After having them over to our home a couple of times, we decided to take the next step, to involve the women.

My next social session was with these two guys. After a couple of hours, I asked, "How would you guys feel if I asked you to bring your wives the next time you came over? My wife would like to have a couple of female friends to talk to. She gets lonely not knowing anyone and having no family near." One of the guys immediately said, "Oh, we couldn't do that. It is not proper." The other guy said nothing so I simply said, "I understand and dropped the subject."

When the time came for my guests to leave, the one who did not reply to my question asked if he could use our bathroom before he left. I said, "Sure."

When the first guy left the other came out of the bathroom and said, "I think my friend is too traditional. I believe it would be good to have our wives meet. My wife also has no friends, so I would very much like to bring her. I, however, must insist that my friend didn't know about it."

I replied, "Your secret is my secret and I would like to invite you and your wife to my house on Saturday."

"Saturday would be fine. See you then." he said.

They came to our home the following Saturday. Ali and Begom Jan Ahmad were there also. This was our first mixed couples dinner and we would all become good friends.

Soon after our first couples meetings, Ali said, "We are friends with two other couples and would like you to come meet them. We are having a birthday party for one of them."

I replied, "We would love that." Thus, our social network had successfully begun. Of all the couples, Ali and Begom Jan would become our closest friends and most important relationships.

After working so closely with Ara I was finally able to push Annie out of my mind most of the time. For all intents and purposes, Ara and I were a married couple in every sense of the word.

We soon developed a routine of nightly get-togethers, Saturdays were international food, and Sundays were excursions in the Land Rover.

Our Saturdays became the most popular activity. Word seemed to spread like wildfire. The result was that there was always someone new who wanted to be invited. That kept week nights filled with meeting new people then inviting them on Saturdays. Our social network was growing better than we could have hoped.

Our Sunday excursions also produced good results. We got two kinds of intelligence very quickly. When we drove through the countryside, our passengers would somehow signal the roads we shouldn't take. This, we believed, identified where IEDs (Improvised Explosive Devices) might be planted. This usually was another confirmation of intelligence we already had. The most beneficial results were that we were able to put our passengers into two classes. One class was just regular citizens. These people always wanted to stay on well-traveled roads. The other class was those who had us avoid specific roads or areas. We classified these people as, most likely, Taliban or their supporters. Categorizing our contacts was very important intelligence.

I had gone to Jalalabad the week before and met with Al Smith. I told Al, "I think we should let Ali and Begom Jan move into the empty main house since we are spending so much time together. Al said, "I think that's a great idea. In fact, I think you should offer it on a permanent basis. One of these days, you will have to leave Afghanistan. When you do, we'll have to set someone else up in your place. In this way, we can hire Ali and Begom Jan to become the primary permanent residents in charge of the compound."

I replied, "OK, I'll ask them when I get back home."

After I got back, I proposed the idea to Ali and Begom Jan. I also told them it was part of their compensation, including all food. They said yes before I could catch my breath after proposing the idea. Two weeks later, Ali and Begom Jan moved in.

Shortly after they moved in, they invited their friend Maryam and her new boyfriend to stay a few days with them. They became regular visitors and close friends.

It proved to be very nice having Begom Jan and Ali living next door. After their move, most of our off-duty time was also spent with them on a purely personal basis. i.e., no business or "shop talk". This resulted in a different relationship. I think it's OK to say that we became family.

Nobody knew it but we had satellite AFN that we enjoyed when we were alone in our private living area.

After a while, we finally told Ali and Begom Jan about our TV. We then watched together and life was pretty good.

A few days later, we received a weather report that said a blizzard would hit our area the first week of December.

We settled in for the storm and Ali and Begom Jan were over for dinner. After dinner, we were watching TV and Ara got up, looked out the window, and said, "Come look at this snow. I can't even see the Jacuzzi." We all went to the window and looked.

Then Ara said, "I've got a crazy idea. Let's go to the Jacuzzi."

Begom Jan said, "Sounds great to me. Let's go."

Ara said, "OK but, this time I want to wear my bikini. Is that OK with you guys?"

Begom Jan said, "OK, but I don't have a bikini."

Well, if you would like to borrow one of mine," Ara replied, "I have one you can wear. Let's go change."

I said, "I'll turn on the heaters while we all change."

As it turned out, the bikini was too small for Begom Jan but she wore it anyway. The bra looked more like band aids than a bra. It only covered a little more than her nipples. The bottom was more like a G string. She was more than exposed, but it didn't matter to her.

I thought, *"Boy, talk about up close and personal!"*

We changed and ran to the Jacuzzi. It was very cold with blowing snow so heavy visibility was only a few feet.

When we got inside the greenhouse, I said, "This is insanity." Everyone had a big laugh and we climbed into the hot water.

Begom Jan said, "This is wonderful!"

I turned on some soft music and we just sat there enjoying the hot water rushing over us.

After a few minutes, Ara asked, "Is it OK if I take off my bra?"

Begom Jan said, "Only if I can too."

Ara said, "OK," and pulled off her bra.

Begom Jan followed and said, "This feels wonderful."

This simple act was the last barrier between us. After tonight we were definitely family.

We all talked for about half an hour when Begom Jan became completely quiet and pensive. Ara recognized her mood change and asked, "What's wrong Begom Jan?"

Begom Jan hesitated then said, "I was just remembering my past and marveling about the contrast with this.

Just think, when I was married off at thirteen I would have never considered being here, doing what I'm doing. I'm bra-less in the presence of a man not my husband. That would have been impossible to even fanaticize about. This is truly life on another planet. How could I be so blessed?

You know, if my father was alive and saw us like this, he would have had us all stoned to death, mutilate our bodies, and fed us to the pigs.

My brothers would do the same. How can people believe that way? This brings us a lot of pleasure and hurts no one. I don't believe it is shameful or dishonorable."

I said, "You're absolutely right and you deserve this better life. We are happy for you beyond your belief. Having said that, I added, "We had better get out of this Jacuzzi or we'll be sorry."

Ali said, "I agree. Let's go."

We left the Jacuzzi going our separate ways and went to bed. I awoke early the next morning. When I was fully awake, I saw Ara standing at the window, looking out and very softly singing.

I said, "Good morning sunshine, and Ara replied, "Come look at this."

I got out of bed and stood beside her, looked out the window, and put my arm around her.

She said, "My God. I would have never believed this shit hole could be so beautiful."

We must have received more than a foot of snow the night before. Everything was covered with snow. The mountains were majestic in their white clothes.

After looking for a while, I put both arms around Ara, squeezed her and said, "I love you."

She said, "I love you too," and she wrapped her arms around me. "Let's get something to eat." We got dressed and went to breakfast.

In the coming months, we continued our socializing routine and continued to expand our contacts.

One afternoon, Al Smith called and said, "Hey old buddy, I've got an emergency assignment in your area. We have to fly you out tonight. Can you be ready and get to the chopper pickup point in an hour and a half?"

I said, "Yes," then told Ara that I was leaving, got my gear, and had a driver take me to the pickup point.

Mission 3—Air Force JTAC Down

❧

T he previous day, a U.S. Air Force JTAC (Joint Tactical Air Controller) went down in a Taliban stronghold area on the East side of Korangal Valley.

This area was the cradle of Jihad, and the Taliban controlled every village for miles around. This area had the heaviest concentration of insurgents in Afghanistan at that time.

I was selected for the assignment because I had the best chance of moving among the locals.

It was February 20th, 2006, the elevation was above 5,000 feet and it was extremely cold. The snow was deep and offered some protection from the cold if the JTAC was able to cover himself in snow.

The JTAC was an Air Force Sargent named Fred Jenkins. He was either injured, or dead, and needed to be extracted if possible.

I was dropped, after dark, near his last known coordinates. This was in extremely rugged mountains with nothing but boulders, caves, steep inclines, drop offs, and snow.

Tribal villages were scattered throughout the valley. Both Taliban and Mujahideen used this area. Additionally, they intimidated the tribes by threatening to use them as human shields. If the tribes didn't hide them, they and their entire household, would be killed.

Sargent Jenkins was definitely in a serious predicament.

When I got there, we were surrounded by villagers and insurgents.

Since I was in my Saudi disguise and if was seen, I hoped the villagers would assume I was an insurgent. At least, that was the theory.

Before being deployed, I was briefed on Sargent Jenkins. I learned as much about him as possible. I was again very thankful for my photographic memory.

Jenkins was a black Air Force Sergeant born and raised in Tupelo, Mississippi. I learned his name, parents and sibling's names, where he went to school, his high school girlfriend's name, and his wife and children's names.

I was given lots of other details that would be known only by him or one of his family members. This information might be necessary to convince Jenkins that I was a friend. In this case, my disguise would be working against me.

If Jenkins didn't buy it, he might kill me when I approached. That is, if he was still alive.

Now on the ground, I had to find Jenkins in the dark. There was no moon and I couldn't see my hand in front of my face but I still had to find him before daylight.

I was also concerned that he was wounded, and I didn't know how badly.

Before I could get my bearings, I could hear activity close enough that it seemed as though I could reach out and touch them. I thought, *"This must be a mind trick. I hope they aren't as close as they seemed."*

Never the less my heart was pounding like a jack hammer. I also knew that I was very close to steep cliffs, but I couldn't see anything but black. One wrong move and there would be two of us dead.

I began inching my way very carefully moving in a circle and slowly extended the circle until I found either Fred or his body.

I was thinking, *"What the hell am I doing here? Is this what I wanted to do when I became a Navy SEAL? Dad didn't tell me about this part. Oh well, I'm here now so, once again, I am repeating my motto but this time it was more like a prayer."* It calmed me down and helped keep my mind focused.

I felt my way in the dark for about an hour, or so it seemed. I didn't know for sure. I, occasionally, heard the reports of pistols and AK-47s in the distance. I thought, *"Why in hell are they shooting at this time of night?"*

At that moment, I heard a very laud report of a pistol. Then I thought, *"Damn, a bullet barely missed my head. I sure hope it is Fred."*

I called out, "Fred Jenkins. Is that you?" I got no reply and, instantly got very concerned. I thought, *"It must be Fred. The insurgents would have begun shooting at everything in the entire area."*

I then started calling out personal details only Fred would know. He still said nothing.

Then I said, "Dammit boy, I'm your honkey brother, and I'm here to get your black ass out of here."

With that, he finally replied, "Don't call me boy you honkey. I'm Sergeant Fred Jenkins, U.S. Air Force."

I then said, "I thought that might just get your attention. My name is Abdul Rahid. I'm a U.S. Navy SEAL in local disguise so don't shoot me. You damned near killed me a minute ago"

I then began asking him questions about his life that only he could know.

Fred said, "Why the hell are you asking me these stupid questions?

I said, "I'm going to keep asking these stupid questions until I'm satisfied that you are really Sargent Jenkins. I asked a few more questions then said, "I'm coming in. Put that damned gun down. Good thing you fly boys can't shoot straight."

"OK, don't be a smart ass," Fred said.

I laughed and moved toward him.

Sgt. Jenkins said, "Be careful. There is a sharp steep drop off near you and don't try to get to me in the dark. If you fall into this ravine, we'll both end up dead. Wait until morning, I'm OK."

"You sure?" I replied.

"I'm down a ravine about 50 feet and it's another two or three hundred feet to the bottom," he said.

"How bad are you hurt?"

"I have a broken arm and a bullet in my hip. I think my hip might be pretty bad. I think maybe I also have a broken shoulder," he replied.

"Are you bleeding?"

"I was but I'm pretty sure I stopped the bleeding. Anyway, it doesn't matter. You can't get to me until daylight. I'm covered enough to keep me from freezing so wait until morning,"

I then settled in and went to sleep. At daylight, I looked around. The first thing I saw was a sheer drop off about 18 inches from where I lay.

"*Wow, If I had just turned over in my sleep I would now be dead,*" I thought.

As I looked for Sgt. Jenkins, I saw the steep drop off just inches from him.

"*How in the hell didn't he kill himself?*" I wondered.

He was lying against a large boulder. It both protected him from view and also kept him from falling further.

The ravine he was in was another 500 feet down. He and the boulder were resting on a small ledge about three feet wide. It's a wonder he wasn't all the way down to the bottom—and dead.

Examining the situation, I quickly realized that getting to him would be challenging to say the least. Even more daunting, was how to get us both out of there and up to the top. There was, at best, a 50—50 chance of getting Fred out, but I was going to give it everything I had to get him out of there.

I knew it would all depend on whether Fred could help or would he be only dead weight. I worked my way down to Fred. When I got to him, I checked his overall condition and dressed his bullet wound. I put makeshift splints on his broken arm and strapped his shoulder the best I could.

When I finished, Fred said, "I believe I located a large ammunition storage dump and their command center. I think there are some high level characters there now. I do know that these guys just sit up here and shoot down on our army outpost. We must blow this place to hell if we can.

My plan was to direct A10 Warthogs to, at least, take out the ammo dump and the command post in one attack. I was shot before I could get close enough to direct the attack. I'm not leaving until my mission is complete so you will have to do it."

"OK. Where is it? I'll see if I can do something," I said.

Fred pointed to the area and said, "You need to get about a thousand yards closer."

"Shit that's right in their front yard. Does it have to be that close?"

Fred said, "Yes and that's not all. When you blow it, they will swarm this entire area very fast. You won't have time to get out carrying me so I'll stay and draw their fire while you get the hell out of here. Do you agree with that?"

I said, "Hell no. First, if I agreed with you, we would both be wrong. Second, I outrank you and that makes me boss. Lastly, Navy SEALS don't work that way. So, we either both go or we both stay."

Fred said, "That's bullshit. That's just plain suicide."

I replied, "Bull shit or not, but we are both getting out or we'll take a bunch of those assholes with us."

Fred said, "OK, but it's your ass. And, by the way, I like your style man."

"Check me out on your communication protocol."

Fred checked me out on his procedures and then I scouted the best way to a pickup point. It was apparent that I would have to get Fred out of the ravine first. I had to inch our way up the ravine to the top.

Two hours later Fred and I were back on flat ground and exhausted. I found a secure place and laid Fred down.

I told Fred, "The pickup point is in that direction about 200 yards. If I don't get back, call for a chopper to pick you up. Tell them to go Northeast by East until they find you. Good luck buddy."

Fred replied, "You too."

I then left Fred and began to work my way toward the ammo dump.

As I got closer, I saw a guard on the compound perimeter. I lay there surveying the compound. As I lay there, I saw a truck coming toward me. I took cover and waited. The truck came straight at me and then passed within twenty feet. It was obviously going to the compound.

This is good. There was a road into and out of the compound. I watched as the truck entered the compound and stopped.

They opened the door and unloaded five U.S. Marines. Then, they led the Marines to a small wooden shack. It had no windows, just a door. They opened the door, put the Marines inside and locked the door with a big padlock.

I knew I had to also get the Marines out of that building, but how?

I thought, "*Man, what a complication this is. I have to get closer and devise some kind of plan.*"

I moved in as close as I dared. As I got closer, I saw two sentries about fifty yards apart with the building centered between them. There was another sentry outside the building door.

"*That's three guys I have to take out. And, I would have to take out all three without making a sound.*"

That meant sneaking up and killing them quickly, silently, and without being seen. This would also mean I had to do it in the dark just before dawn.

I figured, if I could get all three of them successfully, I could give their weapons to the captured Marines. That would give us more fire power when all hell broke loose.

Since I was very close with nothing else to do, I laid low and watched throughout the day. This allowed me to locate all the key targets.

I located the gasoline storage, ammo dumps, and officer housing. Additionally, one particular cave seemed to be the most important. Men went into and out of this cave all day long. I figured this had to be their headquarters. If that was the case, the Warthogs wouldn't be able to take it out. That job would need B2 bombers carrying Bunker Busters.

When I had my plan, I contacted TOC (Tactical Operations Command). I identified myself, gave a report on Fred's condition and my plan to get the Marines out.

I told TOC, "The B2s must come in precisely at 0630 hours and take out the command center followed by the Warthogs and take out as much as possible on the first pass. We can't leave before the raid starts, and I will have very little time after the action begins.

I'll move in, take out the guard, and wait until I hear the planes approaching before I shoot the door open.

Then, when I shoot the door open, the Marines and I will haul ass out just before the bombs are dropped.

Tell those flyboys to shoot straight and give us as much cover as possible on the second pass. We only have one minute to get out of range after it starts. Timing and targeting has to be perfect or we will all be dead by friendly fire," I said.

TOC gave me the frequency the aircraft would use and said, "Wait for them to contact you."

With the plan in place, I had to wait until just before dawn to start the rescue attempt. I would have to take out the sentries while it was still dark. I would have to tell the Marines the plan and wait for exactly 0629 hours when I would blow the door open.

At 0600 hours, I slowly made my way to the first sentry. I was able to sneak up on him. With my piano wire, I pretty nearly decapitate him.

I got his weapons and ammo and then moved to the next sentry.

I wasn't so fortunate with this one. At the last second, he turned and saw me coming. All I could do was to run at him as fast as I could and hope to get him before he could react. As he reached for his weapon, I lunged grabbing and twisting his head with all the strength I could muster. Luckily, his neck broke instantly.

I now had about as many weapons as I could carry.

I moved closer to the back of the building and lay down the weapons and ammo. I spread them apart enough to allow the Marines to easily and quickly pick them up without getting in each other's way. Everything had to go off with no glitches.

"Well, here goes," I thought.

I then made my way around the building. As I got to the front, I peeked around the building to see the sentry by the door. Before I charged him, I looked to be sure there were no others near.

"OK, it's time for action. This is not going to be easy. Surely, luck will have to be with me because it's not possible to sneak up on him. How can I take him out?"

Then, I figured there was only one way. I would have to divert his attention away from me.

I looked around and found a good size rock. If I could throw it to the other side of him and close enough to make him hear it, he would look in that direction. This would give me a chance to get to him before he knows what happened. Surprise was everything now.

It was now do or die. All in one motion, I began running as fast as I could run and threw the rock. It worked and he never knew what happened before he met his Allah and virgins.

I then lightly tapped a Morse code SOS on the door.

Then, I whispered, "Can you hear me?"

"Yes," a voice said.

My name is Abdul. I'm with the CIA and I'm here to get you out of here.

"Who is your ranking man," I asked.

"Captain Jim Austin," the voice said.

I asked, "How many are you?"

"There are seven of us. We found two already here and they are seriously wounded. We'll have to carry them out," Captain Austin said.

I then told him, "I've got weapons and ammo laid out behind the building.

I'll have to shoot the door opened, then you guys will have to get to the weapons and run like hell. Just follow me. Two B-2s and Warthogs will only be one minute behind us then the whole garrison will be after us."

Move your guys away from the door and wait for me to shoot," I said.

When I heard the planes I blew half the door away and the Marines came bursting out, picked up the weapons and followed me.

One minute later, right on schedule, the B-2s came in first and dropped their Bunker Busters. The Warthogs came immediately behind the B-2s and lit the place up.

When the ammo and gasoline dumps went up, it was like daylight. Actually, that helped us even though we were lighted targets.

By the time the insurgents could get their bearings, the Warthogs were making strafing runs on their second pass.

We didn't have an easy run out of there. We made our way to the compound perimeter as fast as we could. As soon as we felt it was safe, we stopped to see what was happening.

I had to confirm that the B2s got the cave and the Warthogs took out everything else. The flyboys got everything they came after. We all did our jobs this day.

There was complete chaos in what was left of the compound. Nothing was left except a squad of nine insurgents, and they were coming after us.

I then said, "Captain, have your four strongest Marines carry the two wounded. I'll take the lead and you and your guys bring up the rear. We've got to make a run for it. We'll chance taking the road because the going will be much easier and faster."

We ran up this winding road as fast as we could. When we got within about 200 yards from Sgt. Jenkins we saw that the insurgents would overtake us before we got to safety.

I said, "Captain, you guys proceed to where Sgt. Jenkins is and wait.

I'll double back down the road. With luck, I can surprise them. If I don't make it, Sgt. Jenkins knows where the pickup point is. You will have to deal with any insurgents that I don't get. Good luck."

"You too," Captain Austin said.

I just then realized that on the way out, I was hit in the shoulder by gunfire. It was only a flesh wound but it was nasty.

I walked back toward the insurgents. I had no choice but to engage them in gunfire.

I found a large boulder just before a bend in the road and hid in wait. The poor dumb insurgents came around the bend walking in a tight cluster.

I figured that if I could catch them off guard I might have a chance. I thought, just maybe, I could fool them into thinking I was one of them.

When they got close enough to see me I casually walked to the middle of the road and waved to them. I shouted, in Arabic, "Americans are about 200 yards up the road. They are carrying two wounded so if you hurry we can catch them."

They then picked up the pace and I just stood there in the middle of the road and waited until they got about 50 feet from me.

About that same time Austin and his guys arrived at Fred's positioned. He identified himself and Fred said, "Come on in."

Just then they heard a voice yelling something is Farsi followed by several long AK-47 bursts.

Austin said, "Everyone be quiet and get ready to fire. We don't know who's coming. The chances are it's the bad guys since Abdul was outnumbered 9 to 1."

It seemed like a very long time but in a couple of minutes later, we heard someone coming. Then, we heard the laud whistling of "Dixie".

Austin said, "Abdul must have gotten them all but let's don't take any chances."

Then they clearly saw that is was Abdul. He joined us and we made our way to the pickup zone. About ten minutes later we heard the chopper. We had made it.

"What a hell these days have been," I thought.

It seemed like a long flight and I just sat there thinking back over the last few days. I've got to admit I was feeling pretty good. All I wanted now was to get back to Ara.

We landed, and all headed to the field hospital. There were teams of medics and doctors waiting. As soon as we arrived, each of us wounded were taken to separate examining rooms.

The doctor examined my shoulder and told me that the bullet was still in my shoulder.

He said, "I would rather you wait and get the bullet out at the hospital in Landstuhl, Germany. They have the proper facilities and there is a lot less chance of infection or complications, if done there.

There is no hurry so you can return to duty. If it gets infected, I want you to go straight to the hospital in Landstuhl, Germany and have it removed. If it doesn't get infected, you can have it taken out at your discretion."

I said, "OK with me Doc."

I wanted to stay around long enough to see how Fred and the Marines were doing.

It's amazing how close a bond can be created when your lives are seriously threatened and you come through so much together.

I saw Fred and he said, "Hi, I'm glad to see you. I want to thank you for getting me out of there."

"You're welcome but no thanks is necessary. You would do the same for me and you know it."

Fred then said, "I'm being sent home tomorrow where I'll undergo another surgery on my hip. The doctor said my hip wound will force me out of the service on partial disability. My Air Force career is over."

"Not knowing exactly what to say, I simply said I'm sorry."

Fred gave me his home address and said, "Please come see us if you are ever near my home. Our home is your home, and I would like you to meet my wife and kids."

"Sure I will. I'd like to meet your family. I feel as though I know them already."

I said goodbye and left to visit the Marines we brought back. I found Captain Austin and his Marines said goodbye to all, except one. Unfortunately, Sargent Danny Williams was in intensive care and could not be seen before I left.

Back to Duty

⁂

I got back to Jalalabad and headed straight to Al Smith's office. I arrived, entered his office, and he said, "At Ease." His voice and manner was formal and different from anything I had ever seen.

Then he began, "What the hell kind of report did you make on this event? I've never seen such a piece of shit as this report."

"What do you mean" I asked with surprise.

"I'll tell you what I mean Commander," he said in a very stern voice. "What you did out there is the stuff of legends but when I read your report, it's hard to see that you were even in the action. I should reprimand you, but what you did out there keeps me from doing it. Thankfully, Captain Austin and Sgt. Jenkins were debriefed and I have that report. With that report, I'll be able to give a more complete and accurate accounting of this mission."

After thoroughly chewing me out, he came around, shook my hand and gave me a hug.

"You did a hell-of-a job out there. When do you want to go to Germany?"

"I don't want to go now. I just want to get back to Alishang. The doctor said I could wait as long as I wanted."

Al said, "OK, it's your call. Just let me know when and I'll cut your orders. Now get the hell out of here and get back to your wife.

A plane is warming up for you. While you are at it get some much deserved rest, and that's an order."

When I got back home I just held Ara for a long time. I had come very close to death, and all I wanted now was to feel the safety of her arms.

For the next week, we just relaxed in our private area. We didn't want any company. I just wanted to be left alone with Ara.

When we got around to talking some business, Ara told me that Begom Jan had already sponsored her into the Human Equal Rights (HER) organization. Begom Jan also introduced to the local HER hierarchy.

Ara told me that Maryam was active in Kabul High Society and that Begom Jan was active in the middle class social scene, at least when she is there. This meant Ara and I could become involved in both social classes. We couldn't have asked for more than that.

I continued moving in and out of Pakistan for two to three weeks at a time gathering intelligence.

Ara got more involved with the HER giving her the opportunity to learn more and gather important intelligence.

Ara and I no more than settled into our old routine when I received Temporary Orders to Germany.

It seemed that Al was more concerned than I was about my shoulder. He also believed I need to take a leave. He was concerned that I had gotten too wrapped up in my Afghan lifestyle. He decided that I should take my leave and cut my orders to Landstuhl, Germany.

My leave gave me 10 days for surgery and recovery plus my 90 days regular leave. It seems that I was to have the bullet removed from my shoulder and take R & R (Rest and Relaxation) whether or not I wanted it.

Germany

In early March, 2006 I left Jalalabad to get the bullet out and get a complete physical at the hospital in Landstuhl, Germany. I had to admit that I was well overdue for a leave and maybe I did need one.

My orders also called for me to take leave under my real name so my medical records would not get screwed up. Additionally, I could not shave my beard because I would be returning to Afghanistan as Abdul.

On March 17, 2006, I caught a military flight to Ramstein, Germany. From there, I rented a car, went to Landstuhl and checked into the Bachelor Officer's Quarters (BOQ). I then went straight to the hospital. I wanted the surgery before taking leave.

I entered the hospital in civilian clothes and my full beard. When I walked to the receptionist, I noticed that every eye in the room was staring at me. The reason was obviously understandable.

I gave my medical records to the receptionist and she told me, "You will be called in a few minutes."

Sure enough, about five minutes later a nurse called my name. When she saw me, I could see she had a strange look on her face.

She just said, "Follow me sir."

I weighed, and she measured my height, took my temperature, and blood pressure.

119

Then she led me to an examining room and said, "The doctor will be with you in a few minutes."

"OK," I said.

The doctor listened to my heart and lungs. Then he poked and prodded before saying anything.

He said, "It says here that you have a souvenir in your shoulder."

"That's what they told me," I replied.

The doctor said, "Man you look like shit. Pretty rough out there, huh?"

"It wasn't exactly a picnic but it wasn't all that bad either," I replied.

He said, "Well, let's get that souvenir out of your shoulder so you can put it in a jar and keep it for prosperity. As a precaution, I think I'll keep you here a few days to make sure you don't get an infection and it heals properly."

"OK by me," I said.

The doctor said, "In the meantime, do you want someone to give you a haircut and shave."

"No thank you. I'm not allowed to shave off my beard and I'll get a haircut later," I said.

While I was in the hospital, everyone that saw me looked at me with a quizzical stare. It made me a little uncomfortable at first but I began to get used to it. Because of the constant staring, I mostly laid in my bed. I was beginning to go stir crazy and couldn't wait until my release.

My release came three days later, and I went straight to a hotel and checked in for the night.

I decided to stay in Garmisch because it had a central location and good hotels. I planned to travel to and from there.

The first thing I wanted to do was to look into the full length mirror in the bedroom to see why everyone stared at me. I stripped completely naked and stood in front of the mirror. This was the first time I really had a good look at myself. I turned around looking at every angle. The doctor was right, I looked awful. It's no wonder everyone stared. It was like looking at someone else. My weight was down to 185 lbs. and I looked emaciated.

I thought, *"I've got to do something to put some weight back on me."*
After unpacking, I needed to go shopping for new clothes.

But first things first. I wanted a wiener schnitzel and a full liter of beer. After that, I would buy some civilian clothes and rent a car.

Garmisch was a great place. The only thing lacking was female companionship. I figured there was no chance of that considering the way I looked.

After checking into my hotel, I shaped and trimmed my beard then headed for dinner and a beer.

I went into the first nice looking gasthaus, looked around, and sat at an empty table. As I was browsing the menu, I saw a familiar looking woman enter the gasthaus. I wondered why she looked familiar but quickly dismissed the thought. After all, I didn't know anyone here. While the woman was waiting to be taken to a table her eye caught me looking at her and I smiled.

As luck would have it, she smiled back. The waiter came, got a menu and she pointed toward me. The waiter brought her to my table. She pointed to the empty chair and asked, "May I?"

"Of course," I replied.

The waiter took her order and she said, "My name is Becky. You don't recognize me do you?"

I replied, "I'm Jon, and sorry but I don't recognize you."

She said, "I'm the nurse at the hospital. I checked you in there."

I replied, "You look a lot different in civilian clothes, and I might add, you look better than I remember."

She said, "That's what uniforms and no makeup will do every time. Speaking of looks, you look much better in your uniform. Do you know you're known as The Mountain Man?"

I said, "Maybe that's why everyone always stared at me. I look awful."

She said, "Actually, that's not true.

Don't forget you were in an Army hospital, in civilian clothes, and have the rank of Lt. Commander in the U.S. Navy. On top of that, you are wearing a long beard. We don't see many beards or Navy personnel here. I'd say that might be a bit unusual but not bad."

I said, "You don't have to be kind. I know how I look."

She replied, "What's wrong with the way you look? Because of your beard?"

I said, "Yes, plus the fact that I look like a skeleton."

She said, "Personally, I like beards and you just look lean and rugged. I like that as well."

Well now, I liked what I heard and asked, "What sights do you recommend I see around here?"

She said, "Oh, there are lots of things to see but before I answer may I ask you a personal question?"

"Sure," I replied.

"Even though I like your beard, it's killing me to know why you have it. How is a naval officer allowed to wear a beard?"

I said, "I know this is highly unusual but could I see your ID before I answer?"

"Why do you want to see my ID?" she asked.

"I have to know who I'm talking to," I said.

She said, "I don't see any harm," and handed me her ID.

Her name was Rebecca Jane Simon, Lt. JG, USN. She was 5 feet two inches tall with a shapely, hour-glass body. I guessed that she was about 38"x26"x36".

I then showed her my ID and she looked very puzzled.

"I'm attached to Special Forces and can't take any chances," I replied.

"I see. That explains everything," she said.

Then, I asked, "Where are you from?"

"Simi Valley, California. Do you know where that is?"

"Yes, I said, I'm from San Diego."

She told me, "I graduated from UC Santa Barbara and went straight into the Army. That's about all there is about me."

Then she asked, "How long will you be here?"

I told her, "I'm here for another 6 days medical leave then starting a 90 day regular leave.

"What's your plan?"

"I plan to spend it touring Southern Germany, Austria and Switzerland."

"That's great. Have you been in Europe before?"

"No, this is my first time and would appreciate you suggesting places I should see."

"I'd be more than happy to suggest some places."

We talked for a while and Becky talked about so many places my head was swimming. It must have seemed obvious that I was attracted to Becky but she didn't seem to notice.

Becky was the most upbeat, cheerful, personality I had ever met. She seemed to only see the good things and laughed freely. I genuinely enjoyed her company.

Then I said, "I'm thinking about going to Neuschwanstein Castle tomorrow. Is that worth seeing?"

Becky said, "Yes, very much so. Would you like company?"

I replied, "Is the Pope Catholic? Of course I would."

I still wondered, *"How could she be attracted to me the way I looked. Oh well, attraction just can't be explained."*

"Where are you staying?" I asked.

"I have an apartment in military housing," she said.

"I'm staying at a B&B named HRC Pfeffermuehle. Do you know it?" I asked.

"Yes, it's a nice place and not too far from me." She replied.

We made plans for tomorrow and had a couple more beers. Then we said goodnight and went back to our respective quarters.

I thought to myself that fortune had just smiled on me. I went to bed but found I couldn't go to sleep. While I lie there, out of the blue, Annie popped into my mind.

I could imagine her standing in front of me, feet apart, arms folded and giving me a stare that seemed to say are you planning to cheat on me? As I marveled at that thought, Ara came into my mind.

Ara also had her arms folded; feet apart the same as Annie and with the same look on her face.

I thought, *"Am I going insane?"*

It bothered me so much that I got out of bed and began to pace the floor. Why am I seeing these women looking so accusingly at me? I seemed to have two additional consciences. Man, that's pretty bad. I paced and paced for a long time. It felt as though I paced all night long but it was probably only about an hour.

I was beginning to feel guilty, but why? Then an idea came to me. Both these women knew me as someone else. I'm on leave and **not** thinking like Jonathon Roberts. I told myself, over and over, that *"Annie is out of my life and Ara was only my job that would inevitably end. I am Jonathon Roberts. Think like Jonathon Roberts.*

Why doesn't being away from Ara bother me more?"

After pondering this question, I speculated that, subconsciously, I never allowed myself to form a permanent attachment. This seemed to help my mental state.

Then I thought, *"Jonathon Roberts is entitled to have a life, especially on R & R leave."*

When that thought sunk in I immediately felt better and both women left my thoughts. I went back to bed and quickly fell asleep.

The next morning, Becky and I had breakfast and drove to the castle. We got there about lunch time.

We had lunch in a picturesque gasthaus just below the castle. It was a very nice place nestled at the base of the mountain. It had a great view of the castle nestled up on the side of the mountain.

We toured the castle and had another beer before driving back. When we got back to Garmisch, it was almost time for dinner.

Becky said, "I'd like to freshen up before dinner. Is that OK with you?"

I said, "Yes, I'd like to change clothes before dinner as well. I'll pick you up at your room. What's your room number?"

"202," she said.

"I'll be there in 30 minutes. Is that OK?"

"Yes," she replied.

I thought back over the day and realized that Becky had kept me laughing all day long. She was a dynamo, a real life Energizer Bunny.

I knocked on her door in exactly 30 minutes.

She said, "Come on in, I'm not ready yet. I'll be ready in a minute."

I went in and sat down. In a couple of minutes, she came out of the bathroom looking great. She had also changed clothes.

As we left, she asked, "Feel like walking?"

I said, "That would be great."

We walked around the town for about 45 minutes until we found a gasthaus that looked good. During dinner, I promised myself that I would be a gentleman. She was easy going and seemed to be a compassionate person.

She told me she was a "Hobby" artist and loved landscapes and old buildings. She was outgoing but not assertive. She was a genuine pleasure to be around.

There was no such thing as a stranger to her, and every minute was a spontaneous adventure. Becky was also a travel buff and wanted to please rather than be pleased. In short, she was very good company.

I was thankful for her company, and that was worth more than trying to push things toward intimacy or sex. Becky was like medicine and just the right prescription for what ailed me now.

The time with Becky was a stark difference from the life I had led in Afghanistan. In short, Becky was the perfect rest and relaxation for me. I just sat there listening and looking at her.

While we were talking, a trio began playing German music and strolling from table to table. We sat there long after we had finished dinner. We talked and listened to the music.

As I sat there, my mind went back to the cruise. All I could think of was Annie. I wondered if I would ever be able to forget Annie, or, at least, put her out of my mind. I quickly forced Annie out of my mind, and my thoughts went back to Becky.

Finally, Becky said, "I think it's time to go."

I said, "OK," paid the check and we left.

On the way back home, Becky asked, "Would you like to go to Salzburg tomorrow?"

"Sure," I replied. "Let's start with early breakfast. Is that OK?"

"OK with me," she said.

At breakfast, I said, "We should be quick so we can get there and back before too late."

Becky replied, "Oh, we can't see everything in one day. The Sound of Music tour, alone, would take most of one day. Why don't we stay overnight or maybe two nights?"

I thought, "*Oh hell yes.*"

I said, "Sounds good to me."

After breakfast, we went back, packed our overnight bags and left for Salzburg.

Now I wondered whether she meant one or two rooms. I guess I'll find out soon enough and figured I would just go with the flow whichever way it went. Well, it turned out that we used one room. We made love that night, but Annie was still invading my mind. I couldn't help comparing Becky to Annie, unfair as it was.

The next morning Becky said, "I'm having a great time with you. If you can use the company, I can take thirty days leave."

"That would be great," I replied.

I thought, "*Wow, how could it be any better than this?*"

On the other hand, I actually felt ashamed of myself for thinking so much of Annie, but I couldn't help it. I honestly tried not to think about Annie out of respect for Becky. At least I meant well. I don't think Becky ever sensed it.

"*What a deal for this old sailor boy,*" I thought.

Then my thoughts turned to Ara. I wondered why Ara wasn't on my mind as much. I quickly dismissed the thought, and my thoughts went back to Becky.

We had a wonderful time and went on to spend the rest of her leave traveling around Bavaria, Austria, and Switzerland.

Traveling with Becky was like a wild horse ride. All you could do was saddle her up, jump on her back, and hold tight. She was simply full of energy and fun. In fact, she could find fun in a hangover. I was beginning to think this relationship could easily turn into something that could last. Then, the reality was that I would be leaving soon. *"Is this going to be the story of my life?"*

Becky and I had a lot in common including eating, drinking beer and sex. We even liked each other's company. The only thing that interfered was Annie occasionally entering my mind. It was as if there were always three of us and that wasn't fair to Becky.

Oddly enough, I never thought much about Ara, and I still couldn't understand why. I decided to just enjoy my time with Becky and then move on, if I could.

Becky, Annie (always on my mind) and I went from town to town and city to city seeing everything there was to see.

We decided to go to Konstanz, Germany on the Swiss border. We stayed in a very nice place right on Lake Konstanz.

I asked Becky, "How about driving into the Alps tomorrow?"

"I think that would be great," she replied.

Believing there was a gasthaus high in the mountains, we timed our departure to get us there for lunch.

There is snow up there year round, and the views were spectacular. As we were driving through the village, snow was everywhere. All of a sudden, something caught my eye on my left.

I commented to Becky, "I must be seeing things."

I stopped the car and backed up. Then I saw what I thought I saw.

"Look at that, Becky," I said.

Becky said, "I can't believe it."

It was a woman sunbathing in a bikini.

"How can she not be freezing?" I asked.

"Beats me," Becky replied.

We sat for a minute then began driving again. We soon saw a nice looking gasthaus.

I pointed to it and asked, "Look OK?"

"Yes," Becky replied.

We stopped, got out of the car and immediately understood.

"It's actually warm," Becky said.

"Amazing," I replied.

As we walked to the gasthaus we went into shade. When we did, it instantly was freezing. It seems that even in freezing temperatures, the direct sunlight makes a person warm. I was a mind boggler.

We had lunch with one of the most spectacular views imaginable.

We continued our travels having a grand time. When Becky's leave was almost over, she asked, "What are you going to do for the next 60 days?"

"Actually, I haven't given it any thought," I replied.

Becky said, "Why don't you just move in with me and operate out of my apartment? You could go places during the week and we would have weekends together."

I said, "That would be great with me. I would like that very much."

Becky replied, "Then it's settled."

We spent the next two months packing as much as possible into weekends. During the week, I would simply drive the countryside exploring and playing tourist.

My usual day was to drive in a different direction until lunch time, have lunch in a gasthaus, and then drive back to Becky's making sure I was back before she got home from work. You couldn't ask for anything better than the leave I had. Becky and I became very close but we both figured we would never see each other again.

By the time my leave was over, Annie's memory was beginning to fade. I had developed strong feelings for Becky and decided to tell her how I was feeling. I had now found a second love interest but this one had a questionable future at best.

I said to Becky, "I have to tell you that I think I'm in love with you."

Becky replied, "I'm glad because I feel the same. So, where do we go from here?"

I said, "I really don't know. I certainly didn't plan this and it's not fair to either of us. I'm committed for the foreseeable future."

Then we talked about someday getting back together but we both knew the chances were slim. Never the less, we agreed to keep in touch. I said, "Where I'm going I won't be able to call or contact you for a year or more. However, I promise to try finding you as soon as I can.

Becky said, "I don't like it but I understand."

I was beginning to think I was destined to remain a bachelor.

The time passed quickly and before I knew it, my leave was over. Reality finally set in when I said goodbye to Becky. We seemed to just be two ships passing on the ocean of life. We both enjoyed the time together but knew it was probably over.

Now, Afghanistan invaded my thoughts like a bomb going off, *"Oh my God, I've got to go back to that shit hole Afghanistan. Well, at least, I will be back with Ara."*

Then, I thought, *"What the hell am I thinking?*

I just spent ninety days with a woman I told that I loved her and I'm already thinking about being back with Ara.

Is something wrong with me?

Maybe I should see a shrink."

I easily went right back to being Abdul Rahid. I guess that explains it.

It's amazing to me how I seem able to just compartmentalize my life. Surely, that is a human flaw of mine. Oh well, if I wasn't able to do it, I would probably go insane.

Return to Afghanistan

I arrived back at our apartment eager to hold Ara in my arms. Much to my disappointment, she was not home. I unpacked, got a beer and just relaxed. I dosed off and was awakened by screaming. It was Ara.

She came home and found me sleeping. She was so glad to see me that she just screamed and jumped on top of me. It almost knocked the breath out of me.

Boy, it felt good to feel her affection. I say affection because we had everything together except real love.

What we had was the kind of love that was based upon mutual respect and more of an affair of the head instead of an affair of the heart. We both figured that most couples lose their passion and their relationships, and ultimately, turn into something like what we have.

After Ara and I got caught up, she said, "I've got some good news. I spent some time with Maryam Alizai. She really is a mover and shaker, a natural leader. I believe she, and HER, could be developed into a real intelligence network.

I checked with Al Smith and he told me, "get involved as much as possible and see where that would lead. When, and if, you are satisfied she can be trusted, we'll expand our relations to include me."

Ara and I quickly got back into our routines. We had Ali and Begom Jan over more frequently, and we also went to Begom Jan's home regularly.

One day, at Begom Jan's house, Maryam was there.

Upon seeing us, Maryam said, "I've heard a lot about you both from Begom Jan."

I replied, "I hope some of it was good."

Maryam then said, "It was all good and that's something special because Begom Jan doesn't say things like that about many people."

We had a great time and just small talked for about four hours. Just before we left, Maryam asked, "Would it be possible for you guys to come to Kabul a week from Saturday?"

I said, "Sure."

Maryam said, "My father is having a birthday party for my mother, and I would like you to come."

I told her, "It would be an honor. We would love to come."

The day came and Ara and I left for Kabul a day early. We met with Al Smith and told Al that we were going to the party. He was ecstatic and said, "You couldn't do better than that. These people are high society and politically powerful."

Ara, Begom Jan, Ali and I were the only non-family attending the party. Ara and I considered this to be a special honor. We were impressed with the way everyone treated us. The party was just like any society party in the United States or Europe. If you didn't know better, you wouldn't believe you were in Afghanistan. There must have been a couple hundred people there. The amazing part is that they were all extended family, related in some way. Further, they were, virtually, all members of either local or national government. It appeared that government service was a family tradition. This social involvement could give us a treasure trove of intelligence as well as becoming more involved in HER, which was an underground political movement functioning right in their midst.

HER

⟡

The HER has a membership of less than 300 members but was slowly growing. More significantly, HER adopted The "Pledge of Independence of 1996" as their charter. It read:

"We believe that all humans are created equally by Allah with absolute rights, among these are equal in fundamental worth and moral status, life, liberty and the pursuit of Happiness.

These rights equally apply to gender, skin color and any other differences between individuals.

To secure these rights, Governments must be instituted among people to secure and protect these rights.

Governments derive their just powers from the consent of the people.

Whenever any Form of Government becomes destructive of these ends, it is the Right and obligation of the People to alter or to abolish it.

We hold that members of the HER, individually and collectively, pledge to keep secret all HER persons and activities from all outsiders."

This group's mission is to actively work for and support:

+ Equal rights for women
+ Education for girls
+ The destruction of the Taliban

HER adopted the organizational secrecy methods used by the Italian and American Mafia to bind their members. Of significant note, they also had their own vigilante group, "JUSTICE".

JUSTICE's mission is to carry out justice when commanded by the head of the HER. In order to assure control they developed very strict rules that applied to all action to be carried out by JUSTICE. Additionally, they trained all members in intelligence gathering, martial arts, and combat tactics.

A few days later Begom Jan told Ara that Maryam would like to meet some Americans if possible.

Ara said, "I'm sure I can set up a meeting with one guy I know. I will ask him and let you know as soon as I receive his response." Ara contacted Al Smith and set a time and date for their meeting.

The next day, Ara told Begom Jan, "I received a reply and my friend said he would be happy to meet her. He wants to meet with her, and you, day after tomorrow at our apartment."

In the meantime, Al flew to Alishang to have a strategy meeting with Ara and me before meeting with Maryam and Begom Jan.

When Al got here he immediately said, "I'm sure you both know how important this meeting could be. I can tell you that we will either be in or out of business after this meeting. Based upon everything you have told me up to now, I suggest we 'Go for Broke'. If we are wrong, our party will be over for good. If we are right, it could mean everything. What do you say?"

I said, "I trust them. I say go. I just can't believe we have misjudged them."

Ara said, "I agree, let's risk it."

Al then said, "I'm going to disclose everything including that the three of us are actually CIA. Are we still OK?" Ara and I both said, "Yes."

Maryam and Begom Jan arrived for the meeting on time. Maryam didn't expect me to be there and had a surprised look on her face. Ara assured Maryam that I was OK. We chatted as we waited for Al to get there. After a few minutes, Maryam and I continued to hit it off well.

Al arrived, and was introduced. After introductions, Al got straight to the point saying, "Ara hasn't told me much about you and HER. All she told me was that you could be trusted and your organization needed help from the Americans. I assumed you really mean from the American government. Is that correct?"

Maryam said, "Yes, exactly. Can you arrange a meeting with an American official?"

Al replied, "Well, I *am* an American official. I will explain about myself and how we operate. After that, you will have to tell me all about you and HER."

Al then said, "Ladies, what I am about to tell you is considered of the highest level of secrecy. I want you to swear on your life to keep this secret. It will cost all our lives if our secret is not kept. Do you so swear?"

They both swore and Al continued, "I am not just an American official. I am the Section Chief of the U.S. CIA and Abdul and Ara are my operatives." Maryam and Begom Jan clearly looked shocked.

"Before I say more, I want to hear about you both and HER."

Maryam then told us about her movement. She said, "I believe HER has something to offer the Americans but we need help. Maryam went on to say that, in addition to human rights she, and HER, were against the Taliban, Mujahideen and Al-Qaeda and would do anything to fight them.

Al then asked, "Exactly what can you offer us and what kind of help do you need?"

Maryam replied, "We offer intelligence. We are very well connected and can offer you a valuable source of information and intelligence. In exchange, we need everything. The things we need most are:

1. Money
2. Occasional helicopter transportation
3. Forged documents
4. Male escorts

I believe the intelligence we can provide is worth a lot."

Al said, "I want to discuss a number of intelligence needs. I can tell you that our help would be virtually unlimited but it will strictly be based on a quid pro quo basis."

Al then spelled out the CIA's quid quo pro requirement. Additionally, Al told them that, on occasion, the CIA would request their assistance on certain missions. "The cost of these requests would be paid for over and above any aid."

It was further agreed that Ara and Begom Jan would be the only contacts between the CIA and the HER. "Is that agreed?"

Maryam replied, "Yes. It is agreed."

Al and Maryam shook hands. Then, Al opened his briefcase and turned it toward Maryam. The briefcase was filled with $100,000 in cash. Al also gave each of them a satellite cell phone to be used for all our communications. Al said. "These must be kept in absolute secrecy. Everyone was shocked, including me.

Al stated, "This is to get you started. There is more as you need it, but we won't simply send you more money. From now on, we will want each request to include how much you need and for what specific purpose. Once your request is approved, the cash will be delivered to you by Ara."

Everyone agreed and shook hands again. Maryam and Begom Jan left.

Al, Ara and I discussed some specific intelligence needs and Al then left. Ara and I fell back into our routine. We liked the openness we now shared with Begom Jan and Maryam. From this moment forward, our Afghan family had expanded.

I, now, had to deal with a new problem. 100 days in Europe with Becky was a constant reminder of the real world. This made it exceedingly more difficult to live in Afghanistan as I did before I left.

The Assassination

A few days later, July, 12, 2006 Begom Jan came to Ara with an urgent announcement.

She said, "We believe there is a secret meeting that will take place between the Afghan President, his Minister of Defense, Head of the Afghanistan military, and the U.S. Secretaries of State, Defense, and the Head of the U.S. military in Afghanistan.

We also have reason to believe the Taliban knows of this upcoming secret meeting and is planning to assassinate the entire group.

We were told that they have managed to recruit a member of the President's cabinet and a member of his personal security guard. The plan is for President's security guard to enable a suicide bomber to enter the meeting place and detonate the bomb.

One of our HER members is the wife of a Ghazni government official that has also been bought by the Taliban. Her husband is hosting a meeting next Thursday at 8PM with high ranking Taliban, the member of the President's staff and his personal guard to finalize the assassination plan. She believes she can prevent the assassination by blowing them up at the meeting if she has sufficient explosives.

Pursuant to that, she urgently requests enough plastic explosives to blow up an entire city block. If we can get the explosives to her, she will place it where it will kill all in attendance. She also cautioned that getting the explosives to her would be very dangerous.

The house grounds has a high concrete wall completely around it. Inside, the walls have shrubs and flowers running along them. There is a courtyard with the house in the center of the property.

We should drive to a side street and walk as close to the gate as possible and wait. She said there would be two guards at the gate to the house grounds. A lady will come to the gate at 8:45 and distract the guards by giving them something to eat and drink.

She said we will have to quietly kill them and then give her the explosives. She will then hide them under her clothing by strapping them to her body and legs. That way, she can place them in the best place without being exposed. Once she has the explosives, we must leave as fast as possible."

I asked Begom Jan, "What about her?"

Begom Jan then said, "She'll be OK. She has her own agenda."

I relayed the message and plan to Al.

Al was a little skeptical, but passed the information to his Highers. Almost immediately he was called into headquarters. There, he was asked about his source and whether he actually believed this story. Al said, "I have no reason to disbelieve her unless you can tell me there is no secret meeting planned."

The commanding officer said, "I can confirm the planned meeting."

Al said, "There can be no question about it. We must eliminate those involved."

The commanding officer said, "Proceed with your plan. If you succeed in taking out the bad guys, we will proceed with the meeting as planned. If you fail, we will postpone the meeting. Good luck."

Al called Abdul and said, "We will do it, but, since we don't know anything about her, I'm uncomfortable handing over so much explosives. You make your own assessment of the situation before handing over the stuff. I'll leave it to your judgment. Obviously, a lot is riding on this."

The next day, Begom Jan and I went to a predetermined point where our car could be hidden and the chopper was less likely to be seen landing and taking off.

The chopper arrived along with plastic explosives and documents then we quickly left for Ghazni.

We were dropped outside the city and had to walk about two miles until we got to the car that had been left for us.

Begom Jan put the address into the GPS, and we drove there through deserted streets.

Even though it was very dark, our headlights could be seen a long way off. Too dark to turn the lights off. It was an uneasy drive to say the least.

The woman that we would give the explosives to had been on my mind a lot.

I, again, asked Begom Jan, "How is she going to get out? The explosive timers don't allow much time for her to get clear."

Begom Jan replied, "She has late stage terminal cancer and wants to give her life to be sure it is successful."

"Why didn't you tell us that before now? I consider this to be a lie of omission and that violates our trust. I'm thinking we should turn around and go back."

Begom Jan said, "I'm really very sorry. We must stop this assassination if we can. I was afraid you might not have helped if I told you she would kill herself."

I finally said, "OK, but I sure hope this is the right thing to do."

Begom Jan then said, "Thank you and I vow that I will never withhold anything from you again."

I said, "I just don't understand how people can just give up their lives."

"We have faith that Allah will reward us in Heaven," Begom Jan replied.

We arrived and drove a little way past the gate before parking. There was nobody on the streets and, sure enough, there were two guards at the gate. We turned off the lights and slowly made our way, as close as possible, to the gate. Fortunately, there were cars parked alongside the fence that we could use as a cover. It was very dark, and, with our black clothing, we moved within about fifty feet from the guards without them seeing us. We got into position and waited.

In about five minutes, a woman came carrying a tray, opened the gate and said something to the guards. They laid their weapons against the gate and she handed the guards the food and drinks. She, coolly, continued talking to them to keep their attention focused on her.

I said, "As soon as the guards are down, we will have to, very quickly, drag them through the gate and hide them along the fence."

Begom Jan said, "I can handle mine by myself. You just get your guy."

"OK," I replied.

I thought, *"How could she do that? Both guards clearly outweigh her. Oh well, I guess I'll see soon enough."*

We got to the guards and Begom Jan, coldly, reached around hers with the dagger and slit his throat. The guy never knew what happened.

At the same time, I grabbed the other one by the head and twisted with every ounce of strength I could muster, breaking his neck instantly.

When he fell, Begom Jan bent down, slit my guard's throat and said, "No offense but I just want to make sure he is dead."

I thought, *"Man, I sure wouldn't want her working for the other guys."*

I grabbed my guy but hesitated to see how Begom Jan was doing with hers. To my amazement, she bent over, almost in a crouch, took him by one arm, slung his arm over her shoulder with his body draped over her back. She then, using her legs, stood up with him. We both entered the gate at the same time.

I dragged my guy to the left and she carried her guy to the right. They were hid behind the bushes in 10 seconds. If I hadn't seen it, I wouldn't have believed it.

We then strapped the explosives on the woman and left as fast as we could. Before leaving, I said to her, "Thank you for what you are about to do. Allah will surely bless you in heaven."

Begom Jan then kissed her on both cheeks and said, "Go with Allah and may you have everlasting peace and happiness with him."

We then hurriedly drove away as fast as we dared. About five minutes later we heard the explosion, looked back and saw flames high into the sky. It seemed obvious that she got them, but we wouldn't know for sure until after the secret meeting. We got back to our pickup point and waited for the chopper to arrive. The chopper came, and we were flown to Jalalabad.

We were told to go to Al Smith's office the next morning for a debriefing. Begom Jan and I went straight to our quarters.

The next morning Begom Jan and I had a cup of coffee and went to Al's office. When we got to the office, Al was talking to his clerk.

"Good morning," Al said.

"Good morning," We both replied simultaneously.

We gave Al the blow by blow of the night before. After we finished our report, Al said, "Begom Jan, I need talk to Abdul about other matters, if you don't mind. You can wait outside my office. We won't be long"

"No problem," she said.

Al then said, "I've made arrangements for us to have lunch with Maryam. Be back here by 1100 hours. We are also having dinner tonight."

I went outside of the office and Begom Jan then said, "I will see you later," and left.

As soon as Begom Jan left, I said to Al, "For the record, I've got to say that Begom Jan is an amazing woman.

If it was ever decided to have women SEALS, I'll put her name at the head of the list.

In fact, if there is ever a dangerous mission that requires only two guys, I choose her to be my partner.

I would, without hesitation, trust her with my life.

That woman is an assassin with the strength of a bull."

Al then said, "If this assassination plan was proved real, it demonstrates a lot because I didn't know about the meeting.

It shows, Maryam is both very well connected and resourceful. As a matter of fact, I want you to know that I asked Maryam to help with a very sensitive matter.

We suspected that a General in the Afghan Army was a Taliban agent but didn't know for sure. We had tried for months to prove it without any success. So far, all we had were suspicions. I decided to tell Maryam our suspicions and who he was. When I told her, she said they had the same suspicions but also didn't know for sure. I then told her I would keep trying to confirm it and, if we learned anything, I would tell her."

Al said, "Do you know that a week later she came back to me and confirmed that he was a traitor. To top it off, she brought hard evidence to bring him down.

I asked her how she did it and all she said was, 'We have ways that I cannot disclose.' I then asked her why she hadn't exposed him before. She said that there were so many of these assholes that they couldn't go after everyone one of them. They simply didn't have the resources and had many higher priorities. 'We changed our priorities because you asked'."

I said, "It's pretty convincing evidence that they are on our side."

"That's the way I feel about it too. All we have to do now is figure out how to expose the General." Al said.

Maryam told me, "Don't worry about him. We'll take care of him. He won't be any more trouble."

"OK", I said.

We then spent the rest of the morning going over things in general and then just shooting the breeze.

Before we left for lunch, Al said, "You may soon be eligible for rotation back to the states."

I replied, "If it's OK, I would rather wait until the winter. You know, the winters slow down because of the cold. Besides, there is much to do right now getting things worked out with Maryam and Begom Jan."

Al replied, "OK. You just let me know when you want to go and I'll make it happen."

I said, "Thanks," and we left to meet the girls. At lunch, I just wanted to enjoy lunch and chat. However, Maryam seemed hell bent on work. It was apparent that she had an agenda.

We all ordered lunch and Maryam started talking. She began by saying, "I have something most urgent to say at this meeting. Our future absolutely depends on trust between us."

We all said, "I agree with that."

Maryam then said, "I want to demonstrate our trustworthiness. I want you to know where I live, and I want to take Abdul and Ara there. You must also know that, if we are found helping you, the Taliban will kill our entire family."

Al replied, "We certainly understand, and will die before revealing this or anything else in the future."

"Good, let's enjoy the rest of the lunch."

After lunch, Al went back to the office and we all went to Maryam's home. We met their mothers who were gracious hostesses.

We then talked about how to work together and communicate. Maryam suggested we adopt code names.

I then suggested Shepard for Maryam and Assassin for Begom Jan. They immediately said, "OK." Then suggested Shark for me and Bull for Al. I said, "OK."

Begom Jan then said, "We should call our agents Fish for men, Minnows for women. For our people, and for yours, we'll use Lambs for women and Goats for the men."

We agreed with the code names then spent the afternoon getting better acquainted.

We met Al for dinner and didn't talk shop for the entire evening. That was nice. After dinner, we said our goodbyes.

After the secret meeting was supposed to take place, we learned two thing.

One, The Karzai meeting turned out to be real and went off as planned with no assassination attempt. It was later confirmed that the bombing killed Karzai's cabinet member and security guard along with others.

Two, the "General" was found in his bed with his throat cut. The killer was unknown but a justice symbol was left with his body.

Over the next six months, Maryam established very close ties between she, her staff and the CIA. The CIA then began supplying money and equipment to the HER.

One day Begom Jan spent the entire day at our apartment just to relax with Ara. At lunch, I asked, "Have you ever heard of Science of Mind or New Thought?" "No, she replied."

I said, "I think it might interest you. Will you let me tell you what we believe?"

Begom Jan replied, "If you believe, I will listen."

I gave her two pieces of typewritten paper and said, "First, read this and then we can discuss any part you wish."

The papers read:

Religious Science/Science Of Mind teaches that all beings are expressions of and part of Infinite Intelligence, also known as Spirit, Christ Consciousness, or God.

It teaches that, because God is all there is in the universe (not just present in Heaven, or in assigned deities, as believed by traditional teachings), The power of God can be used by all humans to the extent that they recognize and align themselves with Its presence.

Ernest Holmes said "God is not . . . a person, but a Universal Presence . . . already in our own soul, already operating through our own consciousness."

Religious Science Beliefs

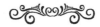

1. We believe in God, the living Spirit Almighty; one, indestructible, absolute, and self-existent Cause. This One manifests itself in and through all creation, but is not absorbed by its creation. The manifest universe is the body of God; it is the logical and necessary outcome of the infinite self-knowingness of God.

2. We believe in the individualization of the Spirit in Us, and that all people are individualizations of the One Spirit.

3. We believe in the eternality, the immortality, and the continuity of the individual soul, forever and ever expanding.

4. We believe that heaven is within us, and that we experience it to the degree that we become conscious of it.

5. We believe the ultimate goal of life to be a complete freedom from all discord of every nature, and that this goal is sure to be attained by all.

6. We believe in the unity of all life, and that the highest God and the innermost God is one God. We believe that God is personal to all who feel this indwelling presence.

7. We believe in the direct revelation of truth through our intuitive and spiritual nature, and that anyone may become a revealer of truth who lives in close contact with the indwelling God.

8. We believe that the Universal Spirit, which is God, operates through a Universal Mind, which is the Law of God; and that we are surrounded by this Creative Mind which receives the direct impress of our thought and acts upon it.

9. We believe in the healing of the sick through the power of this Mind.

10. We believe in the control of conditions through the power of this Mind.

11. We believe in the eternal Goodness, the eternal Loving-kindness, and the eternal Givingness of Life to all.

12. We believe in our own soul, our own spirit, and our own destiny; for we understand that the life of all is God.

13. We believe in the power of our own beliefs.

Begom Jan read it, and then read it again.

Then she said, "It sounds wonderful. You actually believe this?"

I said, "Yes, and many thousands around the world believe and practice it."

Begom Jan said, "Is it possible that you could teach this to me?"

I replied, "No, but we have a Lay Minister in Jalalabad. Her name is Jennifer Barker. I could ask her to teach you."

"Wonderful," she said.

I replied, "I'll ask her to contact you directly. I'll add that you can trust her completely. Jennifer is one of our team members in the CIA. I'll tell her who you are."

Begom Jan said, "Yes, I'd like that."

I continued, "I have a personal motto that I would also like to share with you. I think it could be of significant benefit you. It is *'Failure will never overtake me if my determination to succeed is strong enough.'*

Begom Jan said, "That's a wonderful motto. I shall adopt it. Thank you for everything."

"You're very welcome," I replied and we all parted.

I was, more than ever, wanting to leave Afghanistan for good. I felt the time was nearing for me to rotate back to the states.

I had mixed emotions. I was bummed out that Ara and I would never see each other again, but I was looking forward to finally be getting out of Afghanistan and back to a real life. I finally decided to contact Al and have him cut my orders anytime he wanted.

Al said, "OK, but there is one more mission we would like you to make before you leave if that's OK with you."

Al set up the mission and gave me my orders.

One night just before I was to leave on the mission I was lying in bed and couldn't go to sleep. There was a full moon, and I was trying to sort out the last bits of intelligence we had gathered.

Then, Ara whispered, "Abdul, are you awake?"

I looked at her and said, "Yes."

Ara said, "I want you to know how happy I am that you are the man I was teamed with on this assignment. I think you are the perfect man to have here.

This place is so far from my real life that I feel as though we live on an alien planet, and you are the only human here beside me. Being who you are and being with me has kept me from going mad. I'm very thankful for that, and I love you for that.

You know, I often wonder how I ever got into the CIA and assigned to this kind of life. You have made it worthwhile on all levels."

I replied, "I wonder the same thing. I spent my entire life with a goal of becoming a Navy SEAL. Once I achieved that goal, the Navy became my life planner. I simply go where they tell me to go and do what they tell me to do. Then, I ask what I did to deserve living in this shit hole of a country in such a harsh and deadly lifestyle. I certainly didn't have this in my plans but here we are.

I'm thankful for you as well. And, I love you for that. You have been my life. I hope fate puts us back together somewhere down the road of life."

Ara and I didn't love each other in the traditional sense, but there was mutual respect plus we really liked each other. We both agreed that we had a wonderful couple of years and that we should be grateful for that.

My time living with Ara convinced me that married life was definitely for me. I am surely going to miss Ara.

I was already very tired of the thought of being alone and we weren't even separated yet. Well, I've got to do what I've got to do.

The next morning, I kissed Ara goodbye and left for the airport.

On the flight to Jalalabad, I had time to think about the future. I realized that, contrary to my earlier life goal, I didn't like life as a SEAL or the CIA. I wanted, more than anything, to have a "normal" life. I wondered what my life would be like in the regular Navy, or if there was a possibility of having a normal life.

I received new orders to report to the U.S. Embassy in Kabul. Al and I said goodbye over lunches I left, Al said, "See you."

"See you", I replied and left.

Al Qaeda

⸎

I had nothing to do but lay around for the next two weeks. Then I received my new assignment. My assignment was to infiltrate an Al-Qaeda group working near Saidabad, Afghanistan and then learn exactly where they were operating in Pakistan.

The Defense Department developed a new device that could transmit a signal anywhere from 25 feet to 500 feet, depending upon how it was placed.

A receiver would mount to existing mine detectors. That way, if the transmitting device could be placed near IEDs, they could be more safely located and disarmed.

If they were placed upright, the transmitting distance would have the greatest range. If they were lying on their sides, the transmitting distance would have the minimum range.

The transmitters were made to look like the rocks found in Afghanistan. They were made to always land upright unless blocked by rocks, debris, or depressions in the roadway. The transmitters could be thrown close to the IEDs and give at least twenty five feet warning.

The problem with this is how to plant these devices. They figured that if covert agents could infiltrate Al-Qaeda to place them it might be effective.

After learning where to go, I was to proceed there and try to join the Al-Qaeda element. While there, I was also to gather intelligence data and forward it to Kabul. Lastly, it was decided that it would most likely be a very short time before I would be discovered. As such, I should be prepared to leave on short notice.

My objectives were;

1. Infiltrate Al-Qaeda
2. Gather intelligence
3. Plant as many transmitters as possible
4. Plant GPS transmitters in key locations so the Air Force could destroy the facility after I left.

At the end of October, 2006, I was dropped near the Al-Qaeda camp and from there I was on my own. I now had to make contact with Al-Qaeda and work my way into their group.

It took a few weeks, but I finally made a friend. He was a Saudi from Riyadh. Once he was convinced that I knew Riyadh very well, he considered me his brother. Shortly thereafter he informed his cell leader about me. The next day I was called to meet the leader.

I don't mind saying that I was afraid. There was nothing I could now do but hope that they would consider me one of their own. This is the point of no return. I would either be accepted or killed. This time I felt extremely vulnerable. I couldn't fight my way out. For the first time, I was not in control.

I was escorted to the leader's tent. Much to my surprise, the Chief was Mohammed, the first Saudi I met at the little restaurant in Alishang. The room was full of men, all eyeing me with suspicion. Mohammed and I exchanged greetings and talked for a while.

Mohammed then stood up and announced, "Abdul is a brother and it's a pleasure to see him again. He will be joining our group."

He sat down and continued, "Did you ever find your brother?"

I said, "No."

Mohammed then said, "Neither did I."

We began to talk about the cell group and what our goals would be. He told me, "You are to join with a few other new guys for training." With that, I was accepted into the local Al-Qaeda cell.

A little while later Mohammed said goodnight and I was escorted to my tent.

The next day, the group of seven new guys then entered the training camp to learn how to make and place IEDs. After training, we would place two or three IEDs a day. I would place transmitters or call their general locations back to TOC.

My primary task was also to gather intelligence. I was to count personnel strength, locate ammunition and supplies locations, command posts and officer housing.

During our free times, I would talk some of the guys into exploring the area on the pretext of trying to find prostitutes. This went on rather routinely for almost a year.

One night, as I was radioing my report, a couple of guys mistakenly came into my quarters and discovered me on my radio.

One yelled to the other guy to sound the alarm as he lunged toward me with a knife. I reached for his head as he thrust the knife toward my stomach. As he stabbed at my stomach, I grabbed his head and as fast and hard as I could, I twisted his head, breaking his neck instantly.

Fortunately, his knife hit my AK47 instead of finding flesh. This literally saved my life.

I took off running as fast as I could. A group of new guys ran after me firing their weapons. Bullets were flying all around me then one hit my left butt cheek. A couple of seconds later another bullet pierced my right upper arm. It was also only a flesh wound. So far, luck was on my side. I was also fortunate that the guys chasing me were not very familiar with the area and I was. I easily evaded them and ran as fast as I could toward a predetermined location suitable for picking me up by chopper. As I ran, I turned on an emergency SOS signal. When I got to the area, I hid and waited.

About two hours later, my radio crackled, "This is Blue Jay calling Mole 1."

I answered, "This is Mole 1. I read you."

Blue Jay replied, "I'll make a fast pass then set down.

When I do, you haul ass toward me. We don't have any time to spare."

"Roger that," I replied.

The chopper sat down, I ran to it. A crewman grabbed my arms and held on to me. I was still hanging outside the chopper as we were flying out of there. They finally got me inside the chopper and took me to Kabul's field hospital. There, they dressed my flesh wounds, and I was released.

I reported in and was debriefed. After that, I was told the CIA Chief wanted to see me.

I reported to CIA Chief and he said, "Have a seat. Your Saudi identity and cover is now blown, so you are going back to the Navy. As of this moment, your Abdul identity will be killed off in that raid.

I have orders for your next assignment and have a plane waiting. Sorry, there is no time. You will have to go now because the plane is holding for you on the tarmac. Now go."

He handed me my orders, and I was driven straight to the tarmac, dropped off, and got into the plane.

Return to the Navy

❦

The plane was loaded and waiting for me. I got on board, and as soon as I was seated, the plane took off. Next to me was an Army Major. I introduced myself, and he said, "My name is Tom Graham, glad to meet you."

I said, "I'm sorry for being so dirty and smelly, but I didn't have time to even brush my teeth."

"No problem, I understand," he replied.

I went to the bathroom and washed my face and saw that I was very dirty and bloody. I returned to my seat and after another few minutes I asked, "Do you, by any chance, know where we are headed?"

He said, "Sure, we're going to NAS Atsugi, Japan."

"Thank you," I said.

I opened my orders. I was ordered to report to the naval hospital for a physical, shave off my beard, get a military haircut, and a new uniform.

When we arrived in Japan, I checked into the BOQ, took a shower, soaked in the tub for an hour then shaved. After shaving I saw that I looked more emaciated than before. My weight was up to 195lbs. I was still very skinny and my Adam's apple bulged from my neck. It never did that before. I looked like shit! I don't think Mom would have recognized me.

Three days later, I would continue on to San Diego with a month R&R in Hawaii on the way.

From Hawaii, I was to proceed directly to California Institute of Technology (Caltech) where I would complete a Master of Science Degree and then my PHD in Computer Science.

That sounded great to me. I would finally be back in the real world. I began to fantasize about living again in the good old USA.

My thoughts were interrupted when I arrived at the naval hospital for my physical examination. After completing my physical, I was declared "Fit for Duty" and released.

All the clothes I had were an ill-fitting shirt, pair of dungarees, underwear, shoes and socks. In fact, I didn't own a single thing that was regulation. All that mattered was the clothes I had on were good enough to get me to the Navy Exchange and buy new clothes. I bought everything I needed to pass a Navy inspection plus one civilian outfit. I went back to the BOQ and got dressed in my new uniform. I just wanted to feel like a naval officer again.

It was October 17th, 2006, and the air was already very crisp. I can't describe how good I felt in my uniform. I was back in the Navy at last.

At this moment, I was only sure of one thing, I never again wanted to go back to the life I had been living for the last five years. I wondered what lay ahead after Caltech and was looking forward to 30 days of R & R.

I decided to call the hospital in Landstuhl and see if Becky was still there. I would even fly there to be with her.

I called and the operators said, "One moment, I'll connect you."

"Hello, this is Major Simon."

I replied, "Hi Becky, this is Jonathon. Congratulations on your promotion."

"Oh my God, is it really you?" She asked.

"In the flesh," I said.

"Where are you?" Becky asked.

"I'm in Japan but I'm headed home.

I have 30 days of leave and would like to see you if possible."

Becky replied, "You almost missed me. I'm being transferred to Tripler Army Medical Center in Honolulu, Hawaii. Some duty, huh?

It just so happens that I'm headed for Australia from here. I'm going to the Great Barrier Reef first, then on to Sydney.

I'm sorry but I'm already committed so I can't change my plans. Otherwise, I would love to see you."

I asked, "Are you traveling alone?"

Becky replied, "Yes, why?"

I said, "If you can tolerate company, I can meet you in Australia."

She said, "Really? I'd love it!"

"Give me your schedule and I'll meet you there," I said.

"I'll be on Hamilton Island. It's between the mainland and the Great Barrier Reef. I will be there from November 3rd through the 11th, then to Sydney on the 12th through December 3rd. By the way, you won't need a room. You will stay with me. It's already paid for."

I said, "Great, you can't beat a deal like that. I can be there on the 8th and be good for the rest of your leave."

"Wonderful," Becky replied.

On November 8th, I left for Hamilton Island and looked forward to seeing Becky again.

I got to Hamilton Island late in the afternoon just in time for dinner. I called Becky from the lobby and she said, "Hi, I'm in room 404. Come on up."

I knocked on the door and she opened it and just stared for a few seconds. Then she came straight into my arms and said, "I wouldn't have recognized you without your beard. You look so different."

But, she emphasized, "You are even better looking this way."

Wow, she felt good in my arms.

Becky said, "Freshen up and let's go to dinner. I'm starved."

"OK. I'm starved as well. It's been a long day for me."

"I hope you are not too tired," she chuckled.

"No. I'm just hungry. I'll rejuvenate after I eat," I said.

We had dinner then went to the bar and talked for a while.

Then Becky said, "I know you are tired and I have a big day planned tomorrow."

"What's on the menu?"

"We are going to scuba dive the reef. I hope that's OK?"

I replied, "That's perfect! I can't think of anything I'd like better than that. Did you plan it just for me?"

"No, I planned it for both of us."

I said, "It's been way too long since I've been in the water and I've been looking forward to swimming for a long time."

We went back to the room and it seemed as if we hadn't been apart since Germany. We made love and immediately went to sleep.

Becky and I spent the week on Hamilton Island mostly in the water. She seemed to enjoy diving as much as I.

I was beginning to think seriously about Becky. Could she be the one I could be happy with? I figured I'd just let nature take its course and enjoy our time together. Tomorrow will take care of itself.

On the 12th, we packed our bags and left for Sydney.

Becky had already paid for the hotels for the entire vacation, so I told her that I would pay for everything else.

We stayed at the Sydney Harbour Marriott Hotel at Circular Quay, The Rocks. It was a perfect location and there was a very good German restaurant nearby. We ate there our first night. It seemed so natural for us to be in a German restaurant.

Early the next morning, we took a boat and toured Sydney's inland waterways. After the morning tour, we decided to lie on the beach, catch some sun, and do a little swimming.

I hadn't realized how white and pale I had become over the years, especially my beardless face.

I needed some sun. Becky was concerned that I would get sunburned so she smothered me every minute with suntan lotion and kept insisting that I sit in the shade. By the time leave was over, I was beginning to look like my old self. I was getting tan and had already put on 5 pounds. I felt great!

Becky and I took in all the sights Sydney had to offer.

A couple of days before it was time to leave, I told Becky that I wouldn't get any more leave until I completed my studies at Caltech. I told her that I would call her as soon as I got to Pasadena and had a new cell phone number.

I said, "You never know where either one of us will be stationed so we should definitely keep in touch. I'll come to wherever you are on my next leave."

Becky said, "I'd like that very much."

When it was time for us to leave, I decided to fly with Becky to Honolulu. Then I would fly on to San Diego.

When I dressed for the flight to San Diego, I felt like a naval officer again. After saying goodbye to Becky in Hawaii, I went on to San Diego. On the flight, my mind raced back over the time with Becky. All of sudden, my thoughts went back to Annie for the first time in a couple of years. I was thinking that Becky might be my future, but I knew I would first have to try to find Annie one more time. If I couldn't find her, I felt I could then move on with Becky and not look back.

Even if I found Annie, I had to be prepared because she might be married. Another possibility was that it could turn out that our cruise was just a moment in time that couldn't be recaptured. At least, I felt it would put the matter to rest once and for all.

I arrived in San Diego and reported in.

As soon as I got settled into my quarters I called my sister, Elaine.

The phone rang and I heard, "Hello."

"Hi," I said.

"Jon, is that you?"

"Yep. It's me."

"Where are you?" she asked.

"I'm in San Diego," I replied.

"What are you doing? Will you be staying in San Diego?"

"I'm just passing through. I'm being sent to CALTECH," I said.

"When?" she asked.

"I'm taking a few days of leave and then to CALTECH."

"You have to get straight home, do you hear? You have to stay with us while you're here and that's an order, sir!"

"Yes ma'am, I'm on my way."

"Wonderful, we'll catch up when you get here. I want to hear everything."

"OK. See you in a few minutes," I said.

"Bye and hurry," she said.

I said, "Bye," and left.

The first thing I really wanted to do was to find Annie.

When I got to Elaine's, she took one look at me and said, "My God. You look like Ichabod Crane."

"Thanks a lot," I replied.

Elaine said, "Seriously, are you OK?"

I said, "Yes, I just had a complete physical and everything is fine."

Elaine and I caught up on everything.

Over the next week I made numerous calls trying to locate Annie but found no trace. I searched the internet for hours finding nothing. After the week of searching, I finally gave up figured I could, at last, put Annie out of my mind.

I left for Caltech in Pasadena, California and a full load of classes.

Compared to what I had been doing for the last six years, anything would be a breeze and a pleasure.

CALTECH

ow I wanted to concentrate on school and get to my next
assignment, whatever that would be. Maybe the Navy would
assign me to an engineering job.

I browsed the internet for places to live near Caltech. I wanted
to be somewhere away from the campus and college kids. Being
considerably older and with what I have experienced, I simply couldn't
relate to them. It would be great to just be in a quiet neighborhood
away from traffic. I found several apartments for rent and wrote down
the addresses of the best looking three.

After arriving in Pasadena, I looked at all three places and rented
the one I liked the best. Anything would be better than where I had
been living for the last six years. After unpacking, I went to Caltech
and registered.

Caltech had a faculty member named Fred Williams that showed
me around the campus and provide all the information I would
need.

After touring the campus, he also took me to a small café in
Old Pasadena for lunch. During lunch, he asked if I liked outdoor
activities or sports.

I said yes to both and he asked, "Could I interest you in helping
in the Boy Scouts?"

I replied, "Do you think I would have time?"

"Of course, that is, unless you have other outside activities," he said.

"What would I have to do?"

Fred said, "Actually, we are having an overnight camp out this weekend.

It is a Father-Son campout. Most of our activities are designed for father-son teams. One of our boys doesn't have a father so I thought, maybe, you would be his surrogate dad. Would that be OK with you? After the campout, you can get as much, or as little, involved as you wish."

I said, "OK, I'm good at least for the campout."

Then Fred asked, "Have you done any camping before?"

I replied, "I've been a Navy SEAL in Special Forces for the past six years. Does that count?"

"Are you kidding? Would you be willing to give the boys a lesson in survival?"

I said, "Sure."

Fred was excited and asked, "Do you need a ride?"

I replied, "No, but I'd like to follow you to the camp site. I'm riding my motorcycle."

Fred gave me his address and the time to be there.

We finished lunch and went back to the campus.

When I completed everything I needed to do on campus, I went back to my apartment.

Jon and Robert

❧

Fred called later that evening and said, "I think it would be better if I talked to Robert first. If he wants to have you with him, I'll have Robert call and ask you himself."

After only a few minutes, my phone rang,

I answered, "Hello."

"Is this Mister Roberts?" a voice asked.

"Yes."

"Hi, this is Robert Baird. My Boy Scout leader, Mr. Williams, gave me your phone number."

"Hi Robert, What's up?"

I acted as though I knew nothing about his call.

Robert hemmed and hawed a little and then said, "Do you like camping?"

I responded, "I am a Navy SEAL. How could I not like camping?"

Robert said, "Good, I need a big favor."

I said, "OK, shoot."

Robert then told me, "We are having a father-son campout, and I don't have a father. Mr. Williams said you might like to go with me, so I'm asking."

I said, "I would consider it an honor Robert. Yes, I'll go."

Robert said, "Cool, see you Saturday morning."

I arrived at Fred's around 6 AM Saturday morning.

Robert was already there waiting.

Fred introduced us, and we all left for the campsite. We arrived, and everyone got their stuff unloaded and pitched tents.

As soon as everyone was ready, Fred introduced me saying, "Good morning scouts and dads. I would like to introduce Jon Roberts. Jon has been a Navy SEAL for six years. He served with Special Forces in Iraq and two tours in Afghanistan. Jon has been forced to live off the land more than once and he is going to give us some survival tips."

I was wishing Fred would stop with the accolades. When he finally did, I proceeded to give them a short lecture on survival. After my lecture we played all kinds of games throughout the day stopping only for lunch. Around four o'clock, we started to prepare for dinner.

The scouts were told to go out and gather firewood. The boys then had to get the food ready for cooking over the fire. We roasted hot dogs, baked potatoes, and corn on the cob in the fire ashes. When they were done, we enjoyed a great dinner together.

After dinner, we put a high pile of wood on the fire generating large flames. We sang songs and some of the dads told scary stories.

A couple of the dads, secretly brought bear costumes. They soon began to make soft growling sounds and shaking trees and bushes. Then the growls got louder and louder until every boy was scared out of their wits.

The dads all went along with it and shouted, "What do we do?" The sounds got closer and closer. Then, all of a sudden, the two bears ran from the woods into the campsite.

The boys were terrified! The two dads pulled off their bear heads showing the boys they were not real bears. We all had a good laugh and went to bed.

Early the next morning we packed up our gear, had coffee and chocolate milk, then said our goodbyes.

Finally, I told Robert it was time for me to go.

Robert asked, "Would you come to one of my baseball games?"

"When do you play?"

"On Saturdays," Robert said.

"I'll try."

Robert said, "I have my own cell phone. You can call me if you can come."

I wrote down his cell number and gave him my number.

"You can call me anytime you like," I said.

"Cool," said Robert.

Then I said to Fred, "I've never had a more enjoyable two days. I want to thank you for having me here."

"It was my pleasure," Fred said.

I said bye again and went home.

The next Saturday, I went to Robert's baseball game. I really liked doing this and I liked Robert. He was a very nice kid.

The first time Robert saw my Old Harley he loved it.

He asked, "Can I have a ride sometime?"

I replied, "Maybe, but you will need a helmet.

Do you have one?" He dropped his head down, looking dejected, and said, "No sir."

I said, "Maybe I could get a helmet but I would need your folk's permission."

"I'll ask my grandma if it's OK."

I said, "She would have to call me personally and tell me it's OK." That night his grandmother called. After asking a series of questions, she said, "OK, if you drive very carefully."

I bought Robert a black helmet like the ones I wore and the next Saturday, after the game, I took Robert to the Harley dealership. I bought him a pair of boots and leather pants to match my outfit.

I thought, *"He has brought me so much pleasure that the cost was worth it."*

Robert seemed more than happy with his outfit. He said, "This is way cool. Thank you very much."

"You are very welcome", I replied.

We rode everywhere after that. Robert took to the bike like a duck to water. Over the summer, I went to every one of Robert's games. After the games, I would teach Robert catching skills and how to improve his hitting.

On Sundays, I would pick up Robert and we would take long bike rides.

One Sunday I asked Robert, "Have you ever played golf?"

"No sir,"

"Would you like to learn?" I asked.

"Sure," Robert said.

"Good, but first we need to learn the basics, like how to hit the golf ball from the tee at the driving range."

The next Sunday I showed up with a set of junior clubs and said, "I think these will get the job done."

"Whose are those?" Robert asked.

"Yours," I said.

"Thank you, these are cool," replied Robert.

We looked strange on Old Harley with two sets of golf clubs.

After learning to drive the ball, we moved to the putting course. Once Robert could handle the putter, I asked him, "Are you ready for the golf course?"

"I'm ready," he said.

Then we went to a nearby nine hole, Par 3, course. Robert did pretty well. He scored 52.

I spent every weekend with Robert watching him play baseball and playing golf. Every Sunday night, Robert said he told his mom what he and I had done on the weekend.

Baseball season was over on August 10th. Robert's team came in second and Robert was selected to the all-star team. Robert told me he was going home the next day.

Surprised, I asked, "You don't live here?"

"No, I just spend summers here with my grandmother and great grandparents. I'm going to miss you." Robert said.

"I'll miss you too,"

I asked, "See you next summer?"

"Yeah," Robert said.

Robert and I went out for pizza and talked about our summer together. It was hard saying goodbye when I dropped him off for the last time. I had grown very fond of Robert, and we had become best buddies. We said our goodbyes and I left. I vowed to myself that I would keep up our relationship.

During the next year, my thoughts often went back to the summer with Robert. He was a great kid. Robert filled a void by giving me something to think about besides school and my loneliness. I called him every week.

I thought, *"If I had a son, I would like to think he would be like Robert. Oh well, he's not my son but maybe we could keep a relationship in the future. After all, he didn't have a Dad and I didn't have anyone."*

The next summer Robert was back in Pasadena and called me as soon as he got off the airplane.

"Hi Jon."

"Hi, Robert, when did you get here?"

"I'm here at the airport now." He replied.

I said, "I've checked your baseball schedule. Your first practice is a week from Friday but let's meet this weekend and get a little early practice."

We made arrangements for Saturday morning. I said, "Don't forget to wear your riding clothes.

"Great", Robert said.

We met, practiced a little then had lunch. After lunch we rode old Harley and I dropped Robert at his house.

Robert said, come in and meet my Grandma.

"OK", I replied.

We went to the house and Robert opened the door.

"Hey everybody! I want you to meet Jon."

Robert's Great-Grandparents came in and said, "We're sorry but our daughter isn't here. We're sure she will be sorry she missed meeting you. Robert talks about nothing else but Jon.

I spent a few minutes talking to them, excused myself and left.

I went to the ball field the first day of Little League for Robert to sign up for a team.

Robert got his team assignment and practice schedule. After we found his team and met his coach, he asked me if I would volunteer to be a coach on Robert's team.

I said, "OK."

Then Robert and I repeated everything we did the previous summer. At the end of the summer, I told Robert that I wouldn't be coming back to Pasadena.

Robert said, "Where will you be?"

I told him, I would most likely be stationed in either San Diego or Norfolk, Virginia.

Robert then said, "Cool. If you go to Norfolk, maybe you can come see me. I live in, Virginia Beach, Virginia."

"I certainly will if I'm ever near there," I said.

With tears in his eyes, Robert told me goodbye and we parted.

I completed my PHD, and again, faced a time in my life without a specific plan or goal and still alone.

I pondered a great deal over what I would be doing and where I would be stationed after I completed my PHD.

When I received my orders I was assigned to the Naval Research Laboratory, Chesapeake Beach, Maryland. I still had no idea what I would be doing. I'll just have to wait and see after I get there.

Fred Jenkins Visit

I decided to ride old Harley to visit Sgt. Fred Jenkins on my way to Chesapeake Beach. After visiting Elaine, I would go on to Mississippi then to Maryland.

I called Elaine, told her I was coming and was already on my way. I spent a couple of days with Elaine and her family and headed east on Interstate 8.

I was making good time and feeling really good. It's been a long time since Old Harley and I were on the road. I cruised into Gila Bend, Arizona and stopped to check into a motel. I found a small café for dinner.

I was just finishing dinner when three bikers pulled up beside Old Harley. They got off their bikes and one of them sat on Old Harley. I figured I'd better get out there. I didn't like the way they were acting.

I approached them and said, "I would appreciate it if you would get off my bike."

The guy sitting on Old Harley said, "This is a nice bike. I'm going to trade with you."

I said, "Excuse me?"

The largest guy who must have been 6'6" and weighed at least 300lbs, said, "You heard the man. He's trading bikes with you."

I replied, "That's not possible."

Just then the big guy came up to me with his face close to mine, grabbed my shoulder and said, "You're going to trade or you'll be dead."

I gave him a left hook into his gut as hard as I could. I'm sure he didn't expect that. He instantly bent over, and I hit him with a right hook to the jaw knocking him out cold.

Then the other two came at me. I planted my feet wide apart and waited. When they got within arm's reach, I reached out and smashed their heads together. They both dropped to the ground. Before they could get up, two local cops arrested them all for assault.

One cop said, "We saw everything. Do you want to press charges?"

I said, "You bet! Guys like this need to be taught a lesson."

The cop asked, "Where did you learn to handle yourself like that?"

"Navy SEAL training," I said.

"That was beautiful," the officer said.

I followed them to the Sheriff's station and signed the complaint.

When all the paperwork was done he said, "Thank you for filing the complaint. You can go now and have a good trip."

I got up early the next morning and hit the road. The rest of the trip to Tupelo was uneventful.

I arrived in Tupelo, as it was just getting dark. I found a motel, had dinner, and relaxed. It had been a long day on Old Harley and that could beat you up pretty good. I watched a little TV then went to sleep early.

I must have been really tired because when I woke up it was 8:15 AM. It was too late for breakfast, so I just grabbed a cup of coffee and decided to go to Fred's early.

I left for Fred's around 9:30, and my GPS took me through a very poor black community. The streets were dirt, and all the houses looked alike. They were what were called "Shotgun" houses. A Shotgun house was two large rooms on each side of a hallway that ran from the front door to the back door. They stood on either wood posts or cinder blocks about three feet high. All had a front porch, and some had a wraparound porch. A few of these homes had rooms added, either to the rear, or to the sides of the house. Many still had no indoor plumbing. None were painted. I guessed them to be over 100 years old.

There were many large trees such as pecan, walnut and magnolia. In a strange way, there was a simple beauty to it.

Everyone stared at me along the way. I guess not many white guys ride through here, especially on a motorcycle.

I found Fred's house and pulled off the dirt road into his front yard. There were kids playing in between Fred's house and another. They all stopped playing and followed me to the door.

I knocked and a woman opened the door and said, "Can I help you?"

I replied, "Are you Mrs. Jenkins?"

"Yes," she said with a puzzled look.

"I'm looking for Fred Jenkins. My name is Jon Roberts and I served with Fred in Afghanistan. I'm passing through and took a chance he would be home."

Mrs. Jenkins replied, "Fred isn't home but he will be back any minute now. Please come in and wait, I'm sure Fred wouldn't want to miss you. By the way, please call me Wanda."

I said, "Thank you," and went in and sat down.

I thought, *"At least Fred's house was skimpily furnished and small but cleaner than I expected."*

The kids came in behind me and just stood there looking at me.

Wanda introduced me to their kids. She said, "This is Junior, our youngest and this is Natasha, Ashley, and Amber."

Junior asked, "Are you the man my dad talks about?"

Wanda quickly said, "No, son. That man was named Abdul Rahid."

The boy said, "Are you a hero?"

I said, "No son, but I'll tell you about a real hero I know."

I began, "I knew an Air Force Sergeant that was dropped, all alone, in the middle of enemy territory. His job was to find and destroy an enemy camp. He was surrounded by the enemy and a bunch of the bad guys came after him.

The Sergeant was shot in the hip and knocked over a cliff about 50 feet down into a ravine. The fall also broke his shoulder.

After falling into the ravine, he could barely move. He decided to play possum until they believed he was dead and it worked. He had a broken leg, several cracked ribs, and a broken shoulder.

All the Sergeant could think about was how he would complete his mission. Unable to get out by himself, he radioed for help. The Air Force then sent only one man. That man was told to forget the mission and just get the Sergeant out alive.

The Sergeant would have none of that. He told his rescuer if he hadn't been wounded, he would have been able to complete the mission. Therefore, he asked the rescuer to help finish the job.

The Sergeant said, 'We have to complete this mission because it is a very important target.' He told the rescuer to leave him and finish the job he was sent to do. Then he told the rescuer to, 'Leave me behind and save yourself.'

Well, the job was successfully completed. He wasn't left behind and, in addition, seven captured Marines were rescued.

That Sergeant's name was Fred Jenkins of Tupelo, Mississippi. He's the man I came to see because he is my hero."

"Wow, my dad is a real hero? He never told us about this."

I said, "That's because real heroes don't talk about it, they just do what has to be done."

At that moment, Fred came into the house.

As Fred entered and saw me he had a puzzled look on his face. It was obvious he didn't recognize me.

Fred asked, "How can I help you?"

I replied, "Your old honkey brother just wanted to say hello."

Fred looked at me quizzically and asked, "Abdul?"

"Yes, but my real name is Jonathon Roberts, Commander, US Navy."

"I'm glad to see you sir."

I replied, "You don't have to sir me in your home. After all, we are brothers and I'm not in uniform. You are my friend."

Fred continued to look astonished and said, "I just can't believe you are actually here, in my house. I don't mind saying that I never expected to see you again."

"I told you I would one day look you up, didn't I?"

"Yes, but," and left it there.

Fred gave me a big bear hug and asked, "Did you ever see any of the Marines you rescued?"

I replied, "Not since the hospital in Afghanistan, I'm sorry to say."

Fred said, "I've become good friends with Sargent Danny Williams. He lives in Memphis, and we visit back and forth fairly regularly."

I asked. "Wasn't he the one that was pretty badly shot up?"

Fred replied, "Yes, he's the one. He stays in contact with them all. He said that Colonel Austin is now at The Pentagon."

Do you, by any chance know his outfit", I asked.

"No, but Danny has his phone number. I'll call Danny", Fred said.

Fred dialed, waited for a few seconds then said, "Hi Danny, this is Fred."

"Hi Fred, how's things?" he asked.

"You'll never, in a million years guess who is sitting at my table now", Fred said.

"Sure I can. It's Abdul", Danny replied.

Fred asked, "How in the hell did you know that?"

Danny replied, "He is the only man in the world that you would be so excited about."

"I see how you could guess now that you mention it," Fred said.

Danny said, "Let me speak to him. I must talk to him."

"Sure," Fred said as he handed the phone to me.

I took the phone and said, "Hi Danny. How's it going? It's good to hear from you."

"I'm fine. There are a couple of things I would like to say to you, sir. First, I want to thank you for saving my life. Were it not for you, I surely wouldn't be here today. My wife and kids thank you as well."

I broke in and said, "You don't need to thank me. I just did my job and I know you would have done the same."

"Well, thanks anyway. We all owe you. I want to say something else. I'm very glad you stopped in to see Fred. You should know that every time any of us get together we always talk about you especially Fred. You know, he thinks you put the sun in the sky every morning and hang the moon each night. He always figured he would never see you again. I know this visit means everything to him."

I replied, "That's nice to hear. Thanks. Fred tells me that you might have Captain Austin's phone number."

Danny said, "Yes sir. He is at the Pentagon but he's now a Bird Colonel." He then gave me his number.

"I'll look him up as soon as I get to DC. By the way, how are Betty and the two kids?"

"How do you know my wife's name? I've only met you once."

I said, "Well, I made it my business to learn about you and to make sure you got well. That's how I know them."

Danny said, "You are a very good man sir. I'm truly honored."

I then thanked him for Colonel Austin's number and said, "I'd better let you go. I've got to leave soon. It was very nice talking to you Danny."

Danny said, "The pleasure is all mine. Good night, sir."

Fred, Wanda and I talked for over an hour. It was good to see him again. I finally said, "I have to get back on the road.

Before I go, I would like to ask you some personal questions if you don't mind."

Fred said, "I don't mind."

I asked, "How are you all doing?"

"OK," Fred replied.

"Are you making good money?"

"I get by, but I have to, at times, work two jobs. Things are tough, I only make $2,000 a month.

"Would you be willing to move for a really good job?"

Fred said, "I never gave it any thought and we've never discussed it. I'd like to think about it. What do you have in mind?"

I said, "I know an organization that could use a man like you in its operational test program and your bad hip will not be a problem. However, the job would be in Pascagoula, Mississippi. It's for a Test Technician and is a GS12 pay grade. Do you know the pay for a GS12?"

"No," Fred said.

I said, "It starts around $58,000 annually. That is $4.800 per month plus vacation, retirement and medical benefits."

Fred looked at his wife and she quickly nodded yes.

Fred said, "I can't believe it, but we'll go in a heartbeat."

"Good. I'll have someone contact you."

Fred wrote his name, address and phone number on a piece of paper and handed it to me.

"I can't thank you enough. It now seems shallow to say I really appreciate you even coming to visit us. You've saved my life again," Fred said.

"No thanks needed. Just do a good job in Pascagoula."

"You can count on it,"

"Old friend, I should get going. I'll call you when I get settled so we can keep in touch."

Fred said, "Can't you stay longer?"

Then Wanda quickly said, "Please stay. You can't come all this way then leave so soon. Please stay overnight so we can have dinner together and you and Fred can talk more. It would an honor to me if you could stay."

Fred said, "We understand if you have somewhere to be but, if not, I would like you to stay overnight."

"I guess I can stay but I'll have to call the motel and tell them I'll be staying over."

"We'll have none of that. You'll stay here. Let's go get your stuff and check out now so we'll be back for lunch."

I said, "OK," and we left in Fred's car.

On the way, Fred gave me a quick tour of the area.

"This is where I grew up."

I thought, "*This is nothing but a ghetto. I'm happy that Fred, Wanda and the kids will get out of this and into a real neighborhood.*"

We got back to Fred's house around 11:30 and sat on the porch in rocking chairs. Fred's kids along with some others gathered around us and just sat and listened to Fred and me.

Wanda came to the front door and said, "Time to eat guys. You kids wash up."

We all washed up and went to the dining room. Fried chicken, biscuits, mashed potatoes, coleslaw, and gravy, were on the table.

Fred said grace, and we all dived in.

When we finished, I said, "Wanda, this meal was outstanding."

"Thank you," she replied.

Fred, the kids, and I returned to the porch. We continued to tell war stories which fascinated the kids.

Around 5:30 a car drove up and a man, woman and four kids got out. They came to the porch where we were sitting and Fred said, "I'd like you to meet Wanda's sister Sarah, her husband James, and their children, Jackson, William, Beulah, and Elizabeth.

James and their kids sat and joined in while Sarah went inside.

Fred said, "Boys, I've got to go out back and cook. Come on back."

James and I joined Fred at the barbeque and talked for about another hour or so while Fred cooked.

Sarah came outside and said, "We are ready any time you are Fred."

Fred said, "You guys go ahead. I'll be finished by the time you get washed up."

We went inside and there were folding tables set up in the living room for the children, and the adults were to eat in the dining room.

The food was set up in the kitchen, buffet style, and everyone helped themselves and filled their plates. Then they went to their table.

This was some spread. There were ribs, fresh green beans, and boiled potatoes from the garden, fried okra, and cornbread. It was nothing short of a feast.

After dinner, I praised Wanda and Sarah for a wonderful dinner.

Then, Fred said, "Hey, what about me? I cooked the ribs."

James laughed and said, "Fred, anybody can barbeque. It's everything else that made the ribs good."

I said, "Yeah, that's right, Fred."

Fred replied, "I guess I'm outnumbered and unappreciated. I'm depressed."

We all laughed and retreated to the rocking chairs. It was a beautiful night and the sky was clear. The stars were bright and fireflies lit up the yard. It's amazing how quickly the time flew by. I can't even remember what we talked about.

As I sat there listening to the chatter and laughter I thought, "*You know, these guys might be poor but they seem very happy.*"

It must have been around midnight when James said, "Guys, it's late and we gotta go. Jon, it was a pleasure to meet you."

We all said our goodbyes and when James and Sarah left I said, "I've got to get up to leave at a reasonable hour in the morning so I'd better get to bed."

Wanda showed me to a bedroom and said, "We get up around 6:30. What time would you like to get up?"

I replied, "That's good for me."

Wanda said, "Good, I'll have breakfast around 7."

I said, "Good night," and went to bed.

I awoke the next morning by a knock on the door and Fred asking, "Are you awake? The bathroom is free."

I answered, "Good morning. I'll be out in a couple of minutes."

I quickly showered, shaved and dressed.

When I got to the dining room, Wanda said, "Just in time. Take any seat you want," Then, yelled, "Fred it's time to eat."

Fred sat down and Wanda brought coffee and biscuits. She said, "Butter your biscuits."

I put sugar and cream in my coffee and buttered a couple of biscuits.

Wanda then came in with her arms full. She brought a bowl of grits, a platter of over easy eggs and said, "I hope you like grits and eggs."

I replied, "I've never had grits."

Fred said, "Try them, you'll like them. You put a spoonful or two of grits on your plate then put three or four eggs over them. Then, mix them together. Wanda also has hash brown potatoes. We mix them with our grits and eggs. It's very good."

Wanda arrived with another platter of ham and sausage.

After we finished eating, I said, "I've got to tell you that I've never eaten better in my life. I mean everything—breakfast, lunch and dinner. It was great!"

"Thank you," Wanda said.

I excused myself and packed my bag.

I said, "I very much enjoyed my visit. It's a pleasure to have met you all. I really must go now."

Fred said, "The pleasure is all ours, and thank you for everything."

Wanda came over and gave me a big hug.

She whispered in my ear, "Thank you so much for telling our son that story. He needed his dad to be a hero, I will forever be grateful."

"I just told him the truth. He deserved to know."

I left for Maryland and turned my thoughts to what my job might be. Actually, I had no idea.

I thought, *"What the hell kind of job is in a research center? The only thing that kept coming into my mind was Security Guard. It didn't seem as though my experience had a place in research."*

The Naval Research Laboratory

I reported to the Naval Research Laboratory, Laboratory for Computational Physics and Fluid Dynamics Division, Chesapeake Beach, Maryland on October 8, 2008 still having no idea what my job would be.

As far as I knew, nothing in research could utilize my training or experience. Additionally, I had no experience that had anything to do with my education. How would that qualify me in any way? I was puzzled to say the least.

Upon checking in, I was told to report to Rear Admiral Michael (Mike) Gentry in building 101, room 1412 at 0800 tomorrow.

I went back to my hotel room still trying to imagine what my assignment would be. I soon began to feel stir crazy so I went for a walk. I spent the rest of the day wandering around to kill time. It was a very long day, and I was glad to see it was time for bed.

After breakfast the following day, I went to Admiral Gentry's office. When I arrived, I was told, "Go in, he's expecting you."

I entered, stood at attention, saluted and said, "Commander Jonathon Roberts reporting sir."

He stood up, walked around his desk, shook my hand and said, "Welcome, have a seat," and motioned to the couch in his office.

"Care for a cup of coffee?"

"Yes, thank you," I replied.

Admiral Gentry said, "I'll bet you're wondering why you are here of all places."

"Something like that," I said.

"I have a long, but necessary, story to tell you so take off your coat and relax."

"Yes sir," I said and pulled off my coat and sat down.

Admiral Gentry said, "First, let me tell you that you have been specially selected for this assignment."

Now I was really curious. I thought, *"How could this be? Did they have me confused with someone else? Are they just plain stupid?"*

He continued, "Your SEAL training and the experience you have gained with the SEALS, CIA and involvement with multinational forces in Iraq and Afghanistan give you some pretty unique qualifications. Additionally, your fluency in eight languages had a lot to do with your selection. Last, but not least, your formal engineering education is the frosting on the cake as far as we are concerned.

We know you haven't used your education yet and have no engineering experience. We, however, consider that a plus. This combination of your SEAL experience and no engineering work experience is exactly what we wanted. Any questions so far?"

"Yes sir. How is my having no engineering experience a plus?" I asked.

He replied, "We are working on an extremely classified project with hardware and software never seen outside of this project. We believe your lack of engineering experience provides you with basic engineering knowledge that has not been clouded by old design methods. This means you can bring a fresh set of eyes and ideas to the table. Your real, hands on, combat experience with a variety of weapons and hardware is a major benefit."

I said, "I never looked at it that way. I think I'm beginning to understand."

Admiral Gentry said, "This is a voluntary assignment. That means all you have to do is say no thanks, and you can leave and await other orders. If you accept this assignment, you will be back in the CIA, under a new covert identity, and working as a civilian.

I would also add that this is one of the most important jobs in the world right now.

There is no danger but the job requires Manhattan like security. We know you wanted to be back in uniform, but you will have to commit to four years here if you accept. All I can tell you at this time is that you will become a member of an elite project for the next few years.

Before you decide, there is someone in the next office, who would like to meet you."

Admiral Gentry then opened the door to another office and we went in. There we were met by none other than The President. The President extended his hand and said, "Captain Roberts, it is a pleasure to meet you. I've heard a lot of good things about you."

"Thank you, sir, the pleasure is mine," I replied.

Then the President said, "Captain Roberts, it is important to this nation and to me, personally, that you accept this assignment. We feel that you are especially qualified to do what we need to have done, and I hope you will accept. In addition, I want to emphasize that this IS NOT a political appointment. It is nonpolitical, and your service is greatly needed by your country."

I replied, "I accept sir."

"Thank you Captain Roberts. I'm sorry, but I am on a very tight schedule and have to go now. Admiral Gentry will give you your orders and everything you need."

The President then left the room, and Admiral Gentry and I returned to his office.

Admiral Gentry asked, "Do you have any comments?"

"Yes sir. The President called me Captain, but I'm a Commander."

Admiral Gentry explained, "No, the President promoted you to Captain effective with your acceptance of this assignment, and he assumed you would accept.

Effective 8 June 2012, you will be assigned to Kennedy Irregular Warfare Center in Suitland Federal Center, MD. There, you will join a group of military and civilian personnel that have been assembled to form a 'Warfare Think Tank.'

There have been new technological developments that promise to make the way war is now conducted obsolete. Also, new products have been developed that are beyond the current state of the art and are known to no one outside this program. The major problem now is that these and new products must be modified to work with the new system. The Think Tank must figure out how to use these, products currently in the development, as well as those that will come out of the think tank process in the future.

Ten years ago, The U. S. Government funded this program to develop a wide variety of new hardware and software to be used by the new system.

The group's objective is to develop a new concept of warfare around new technology and to identify other new products to develop. Do you have any questions?"

I replied, "No questions, sir. Sounds more like fun than a job."

The Quick Fox Program

❧

Admiral Gentry said, "You should know the whole story from the beginning. There is no short cut so here goes.

The name of the program is 'Quick Fox.' The prime contractor for the program is Multitronics Systems Corporation. They are located in Chesapeake, Virginia.

Multitronics has developed new technology that has the promise of revolutionizing military command and control across all fields of combat—ground, sea, air and space.

Additionally, the system immediately translates all major languages and their dialects, slangs and colloquialisms.

Shortly after 9/11, 2001, The U.S. Government formed the largest group of world experts since the formation of NASA and authorized the Quick Fox Program.

To support this effort, massive data storage facilities are being built in strategic locations around the world. Each facility can literally store all known knowledge.

These locations are top secret. Even the people who built them and those who are now operating them don't know what they are.

Only a select few people will know everything, and you are one of those select few.

The program directly employs more than one hundred thousand people. In addition, they have design teams located in several allied countries.

Everyone operates on a strict need-to-know basis. No one knows who the others are nor do they know what anyone else is working on.

Each piece of hardware to be developed will be farmed out to contractors worldwide. The individual items are then shipped to Multitronics where they are individually tested, then coupled with its mating piece of hardware, and tested together. When all elements have been built and tested, they will be integrated into one gigantic computer system.

Multitronics has a prototype system that has been completed. The large task is still ahead of us before we have the prototype system become a fully functioning system.

The system receives input from all known military and civilian hardware. The system analyzes and communicates back to all inputters in their language simultaneously.

At the same time, it allows both centralized and decentralized command decisions based upon who is in the best position to command all under strict authority management and control.

The system immediately recommends where the decision should be made, however, central authority can still override the system.

The system is, for the first time, electronically stealthy. It uses frequencies beyond any used by known military or civilian hardware. This offers a complete change in how war is conducted as well as homeland security.

In the beginning, Multitronics specialized in guidance systems. Then it branched into gyroscopic control, magnetic servo products, and robotics.

The company was founded by Randolph Jackson after retiring from the Navy as a Captain. The interesting part is that of Jackson and his daughter. More specifically, it's about his daughter. That's because she is the Manager of the Quick Fox Program. I'll just tell her story and you will get the complete picture.

Mary Ann Jackson

Mary Ann Jackson was born August 12th, 1978 in Oceanside, California. Mary's mother, Dorothy, married Mary's step-father, USN Captain Randolph (Randy) Jackson, on Jun 21, 1980 when Mary was 2 years old. Randy had no children. He and Dorothy never had a child between them. This left Mary as an only child.

Being an only child, Mary had to be a mother's girl. This meant she would be taught all the feminine things; cooking, sewing, dancing, music, including ballet and piano, style, and grace.

Mary was also very athletic, a real tomboy at heart so she also became a daddy's girl to Randy.

Randy and Dorothy were avid swimmers, and both were certified scuba divers. They were, in fact, into all water sports. Mary was also into softball, swimming, and track in high school. Randy and Dorothy began to groom Mary to eventually manage Randy's company.

Randy graduated from MIT with a degree in Electrical Engineering. By the time he graduated he had decided to make the U.S. Navy his career.

Randy entered the Navy and became an FA-18 pilot. Randy's Navy duty was in the Atlantic fleet, and most of it was stationed at Norfolk, VA.

Randy had three loves in his life—his family, flying and engineering. Randy combined his love for flying and engineering into his hobby. He took up remote controlled model airplanes. Additionally, he kept himself abreast of advances in technology.

This hobby also became Mary's favorite pastime. She and Randy spent hour after hour making and flying model airplanes and cars.

Randy soon became frustrated with the crudeness of existing remote control systems. He began tinkering with his control units trying to improve their control characteristics. The more Randy tinkered, the more he longed for a better system. He had a few ideas about improving the remote controls and decided to build his own controller. This led to an elaborate, but better, remote control unit. After numerous modifications and more tinkering, he had a vastly improved control unit. Randy, however, was not satisfied. Now, the weakness was the model itself.

Randy now had a very advanced ground station but there were no existing models capable of matching the capabilities of his remote control ground station. Randy then had no alternative but to start working on a new model design.

It was now eleven years later. All this time, Mary had been at Randy's side helping him do research, design, and build models and controllers. Throughout the process, Randy actually taught Mary electronic fundamentals and mechanical design.

By now it was 1989, and Randy retired from the Navy.

Randy found employment with Consolidated Robotics as an Engineer.

As a result of his and Mary's combined hobby work, Randy patented the remote control ground station, guidance software, and two robotic servo units in 1990.

In 1991, Randy founded his own company, Multitronics Systems Corporation in Chesapeake, Virginia.

Randy and Mary worked throughout these years studying robotics in an attempt to make a model capable of working with their

183

ground station. During the upcoming years there were significant breakthroughs in miniaturization and robotics.

Randy and Mary worked feverishly to build a new ground station and their model airplane before Mary graduated from high school. They did it, and the day had come for their first test flight.

Randy, Dorothy, and Mary went to the airfield and set up their ground station. The controls were tested on the ground and then, Randy gave the remote control to Mary and told her to take it up. Mary gave the plane the throttle and up it went. Mary began putting the plane through maneuvers and exclaimed, 'Its wonderful dad. Here, you try it.'

She gave the control to Randy. Everything worked better than either had hoped. They had reached a major milestone that would change their lives forever.

Graduation from high school was a little anti-climactic after the excitement of their hobby achievement. This remote controller and model improvements would lead to new defense products for Multitronics.

Having caught the engineering bug from their years of developing their model controller, Mary had decided on an engineering degree from MIT.

Randy then planned to adopt Mary because he loved her as if she was his own. Doing so at this time might confuse her educational records. They decided to wait until she finished MIT to legally change her name.

He wanted Mary to carry his name when she began her career in the company. Randy already had a job planned for Mary in his company after her graduation. She was to head up a new department for advanced guidance.

Unfortunately, Randy died April 13, 1999 just prior to Mary's graduation. Randy's stock in the company was left to Mary and Dorothy making them the largest stockholders. Together, they had controlling interest in Multitronics.

Mary and Randy loved each other very much and remained very close until Randy's death.

Mary graduated from MIT and continued to earn a Master's Degree in Computer Sciences and a PHD in Military Command and Control Systems Technology.

She began her career as an electrical engineer for Multitronics, even though she and Dorothy owned controlling interest in the company.

Her new department was the lynchpin of two new government top secret projects. One is to develop a super computer system based upon Randy's remote control computer and the other is the development of an electromagnetic stealth shield for attack helicopters for the U.S. Navy.

Before Randy's death, the company had been selected the prime contractor for the largest government program since NASA was formed, and it carried a level of secrecy not seen since the Manhattan Project during WWII.

Over the next few years, Mary's employment was in the development of weapon systems that coordinate multi force inputs to manage a theater of war.

Mary is the top expert in her field and has extensive knowledge of systems programming.

Mary lives in Virginia Beach, Virginia."

Admiral Gentry concluded the story by saying, "Mary is quite an extraordinary young lady. Mary is a lady of the first order. She is a highly intelligent, charismatic, and self-assured woman. She is warm and likeable but reserved. Her dress is always impeccable and business like. Mary is pragmatic and analytical. She would be a valuable friend and a formidable enemy. You will find her very approachable and easy to work with. She can, however, be the Rock of Gibraltar when she sets her mind on something. Believe me, she is no pushover, so never underestimate her.

I think that just about covers Mary Jackson. The rest, you will just have to discover for yourself."

Our meeting was concluded and, Admiral Gentry handed me my orders along with new identity papers. I would now be known as civilian Thomas Bennett.

Admiral Gentry said, "I'm glad to have you on board Mister Bennett. Good luck."

I said, "Thank you sir," and left.

The Warfare Think Tank

❧

T he following Monday, I joined the Navy Warfare Think Tank team. The team had its offices in the Naval Research Laboratory in Chesapeake Beach, Maryland.

I reported in and, much to my surprise, I was simply turned over to my own personal administrative assistant.

She came out and said, "Welcome Mister Bennett, I am Janice Murphy and I am your Personal Administrative Assistant."

I replied, "I'm pleased to meet you, Janice."

"Please call me Jan."

"OK, Jan."

Jan looked to be in her late fifties. After I got settled into my office, Jan took me around and introduced me to the team. In all, there were 24 of us on my team.

Everyone operated under a fictitious name, and we knew nothing about each other's backgrounds except their area of expertise. That made it better to explore out of the box perspectives, and everyone could question anything or make any kind of statement or theory.

Jan then told me there were four other rooms like this one. That made 96 team members. These are backed up by experts and design teams totaling 956 members. She also said there were 8 countries represented, and that I would probably not be able to detect who was from what country. All spoke impeccable, accent free, English. You couldn't even tell the English from the Americans. Their ages ranged from the youngest at 31 (that's me) and the oldest at 85. There were 26 women and 94 men. There were 2 members for each specialty and no two in the specialty were from the same country. That maximizes the diversity of views.

When we returned to my office, Jan gave me some basic reading material and said this is all you get to know. Things will develop as time and involvement moves forward. The project doesn't want to influence or bias your thoughts. This ensures that your mind is completely open.

After my settling in, all I wanted to do was to call Jim Austin. I dialed his number and after only two rings the voice said, "Colonel Austin here, how can I help you?"

Hello Colonel Austin, this is Captain Jonathon Roberts, US Navy. I met you in Afghanistan. You knew me as Abdul Rahid in Afghanistan. How are you?"

I heard him say, "For heaven's sake, hello. I don't know why, but I never thought I would ever hear from you."

I replied, "Never say never."

Austin then said, "It's good to hear from you. How did you get my number?"

"I got it from Sargent Danny Williams when I visited Fred Jenkins."

"Hey man, it's a pleasure to talk to you. Where are you?"

"I've just been assigned to the US Naval Research Laboratory in Chesapeake Beach, Maryland, and I'd like to come down and have dinner with you and your wife."

"Anytime. That would be great," Austin replied.

"OK, let's put it on our calendars." I said.

We set the date for a week later and hung up.

I read that the objective of the Think Tank's strategic plan is to lay out the way all elements of the U.S. and Allied forces would connect into the Quick Fox System to maximize allied offenses and defenses.

The other objective is to reduce collateral damage to both civilians and property. Actually, there were numerous sub-objectives to ponder such as elimination of conventional weapons, reduce size, reduce power requirements, increase power sources, make things faster, and many more.

The system, as envisioned, required the development of many new pieces of hardware, each with its own software in order to interface with the system. It will be a giant web of hardware, all interconnected, and interdependent. New operating procedures must be written, tested, published, and personnel trained.

The acceptance testing on the main computer system would be done under strict secrecy. System testing would be done by Multitronics at Brown Field, California, near San Diego.

There will be two teams; one is the Multitronics Test Team and the other is the Government Acceptance Team represented by each military branch, Homeland Security, and Israel.

Once accepted, the final phase will be carried out, independently, by each military branch and all allied military forces.

Each will integrate their modified and newly developed products. They will also train their personnel.

This phase is planned to be completed within five years after acceptance in California.

My briefing was completed and Jan said, "Well, all you have to do now is get started."

We arrived back at the office, and I sat down and tried to digest everything I saw and heard. Then, it hit me. I still have no damned idea what I'm supposed to do. All I knew was the team met every day in a very large room. The next morning I went to the meeting room, found my place and sat down.

We had a permanent place at the huge round table. Each had their own laptop computer and behind each of us was our own white board. The white board was able to print anything written or drawn on it. I sat down and waited. Nobody seemed to notice that I had sat down. I just listened to the discussions taking place.

For a while, everyone was discussing a single topic. Then a guy began a completely different discussion resulting in two discussions at the same time. I wondered how they ever got together on a single subject. The entire day was spent just listening. I said nothing and no one acknowledged that I was there.

On my second day, right after lunch, I still hadn't said a word when a guy asked my opinion about what he had just said. Embarrassed, I said, "I'm sorry but I was listening to someone else."

"No problem," he said and he went back to his discussion.

I was listening to a discussion when a new technical term was used. Without thinking, I interrupted and asked, "What was that term?"

The person said, "It's a new material developed by the British. I'll bring some reading material on it tomorrow, but you can find a little more on the internet."

Well, it went on like this every day. I slowly assimilated with the group and began to know each member.

Many of us had a lot in common but, in many areas, had diametrically opposed viewpoints. I was amazed how much was learned from debating opposing viewpoints. It also surprised me how often minds were changed.

The day for my dinner with Jim Austin came, and I decided to go to Jim's office first. When I got there, I went into the office area and asked the receptionist to see Colonel Austin. The receptionist pointed to his office and said he's expecting you.

As I walked toward his office, I couldn't believe my eyes. I saw Annie sitting at the desk outside his office. I stopped dead in my tracks. I thought my heart had stopped. I just stood there. If anyone noticed, I must have looked foolish. When I caught my breath, my heart started racing and the blood surged through my body. I thought, "Jonathon Roberts get control of yourself. You are a Captain in the United States Navy, in uniform and in a military facility."

I slowly began to move toward her. As I walked, every minute of our month together flashed through my mind. I had, finally, succeeded in pushing Annie out of my mind, but it was all back now.

My mind came back to the moment, and I was excited to find her. I reminded myself to maintain my calm.

I then wondered, *"What is she doing here?"*

When I got to her desk I calmly said, "Hi Annie."

"Sorry, my name is Angie not Annie," the woman said.

I couldn't believe that it wasn't Annie, but the girl sure could pass for Annie's twin. Since it has been fourteen years, I just figured my mind was playing tricks on me. I guess it was more wishful thinking than looking alike. Never the less, she sure looked like my Annie.

I must have had a strange look on my face because she said, "Is something wrong?"

"No. My heart just stopped for a minute. It's just that you could pass for a twin to an old girlfriend, and I thought I had found her again", I said.

She smiled and said, "Well, I hope you find her one day. Go on in."

Jim and I greeted each other, talked for a couple of minutes, then left for dinner.

We had dinner at Morton's in Georgetown. Jim introduced me to his wife, Cindy and she said, "It's very nice to meet you. I've heard a lot about you."

We had barely sat down when Jim said, "I've got to thank you on my behalf and that of my Marines. What you did was over the top and miraculous."

"You are very welcome but you know I had no choice. I just did what I had to do."

"No, you had a choice and most anyone else would have chosen the easier way. There are seven Marines and one Air Force Sargent who would not have made it back without you. That's a fact," Jim said.

"Enough said. Let's talk about pleasant things," I said.

Cindy quickly replied, "Now, I can't think of anything more pleasant than hearing about how I still have my husband."

We had a great dinner, and Jim filled me in on all his Marines and where they were now.

I told him about Fred Jenkins, and, around 11PM, we left for our homes.

Back at work, the group studied hundreds of new pieces of hardware to see if it added to our capabilities.

We also examined every new technological breakthrough to determine whether or not it could advance our military capacity to win.

The team had drawn up technical specifications for many new products that needed to be developed.

In addition, every existing piece of military hardware was studied for its suitability for use in the new suite of hardware. After I was there for six months, I was fully integrated into the team discussions.

Then, a new team was set up. This would be a team consisting of only 9 members. The designation for this team was simply "Team 1". Team 1's responsibility was to oversee the entire Warfare Think Tank and its 860 members.

Team 1 was the management team that would decide the final strategy and suite of hardware and software. To my amazement, I was selected to head up Team 1.

New products were developed, existing products were modified, upgraded, and tested. The team continued this activity for two more years. By the end of the fourth year, the overall military strategy was completed and all initial hardware was selected. It was nearing time for testing the Multitronics system which would be the heart of the new military.

The design phase was now complete and the Test Phase began.

The Quick Fox Project

❧

My boss called me to his office and said, "On April 27, 2012, the Warfare Think Tank will be disbanded and everyone will be reassigned.

You are now assigned to the Office of Technology, Innovation and Acquisition (OTIA), Brown Field California. This office is part of the Office of Air and Marine (OAM). You will manage the 'Project Quick Fox' Acceptance Team.

Your jurisdiction includes all military personnel located or assigned to the Brown Field operation.

The OTIA is a government civilian organization and will be the project's cover. You should thoroughly familiarize yourself with these organizations and their responsibilities.

Any discussions with outsiders will be as a civilian employee under contract to this organization. Our cover story is that we are developing technology for border security.

The Multitronics main design team, as well as the overall management of the Quick Fox program, is located in Chesapeake, Virginia, but there is a small team of civilians already working here. Your team's job is to monitor all testing for compliance. You will, ultimately, be responsible for accepting the system.

One of your other major tasks is to be the Government's liaison with Multitronics Systems Corporation, the program's prime contractor. As part of our cover, all military personnel work as part of Multitronics' team of civilian engineers.

Therefore, all military personnel will be issued fabricated identities, including education and civilian employment histories. All military personnel will only wear civilian clothing. Nothing military, including your under wear. No class rings. No military anything.

All work communications outside the base must be made on secure landline phones or secure cell phones.

Each of you will be given your own secure landline number for work related calls. Non-traceable cell phones will be issued to you for personal calls. You are to immediately discontinue your old cell phone numbers. No exceptions to these rules are authorized.

The Program Manager, Mary Jackson, has overall authority for the project. Jackson also manages the Chesapeake design team and is a 'hands on' systems engineer. You and Mary Jackson must resolve all test issues uncovered at Brown Field. All issues at Brown Field will first be elevated to Jackson. You will work with her to resolve the issue. If you and Jackson fail to reach agreement, you both are to independently escalate the issue to higher authority. In your case, it is directly to The Navy Chief of Staff.

Unresolvable issues at Brown Field will be officially elevated along with a complete written report clearly stating your case. Jackson is then required to officially elevate your report along with her written report, rebuttal and recommendations. Any unresolved issues with military personnel will be elevated directly to the Secretary of that service. Any unresolvable issues with Customs and Border Protection personnel will be elevated to the Director of Homeland Security.

These arbiters are only two levels below The President of the United States, so don't let there be unresolved issues! If it does happen, someone's head will roll, including yours."

My boss then said, "Well, that concludes my speech. Do you have any questions?"

"When do I go?" I asked.

"As soon as you can pack up. It's been a privilege working with you. Take care of yourself," he said.

"Same here, I'll see you before I leave."

He gave me my orders, we shook hands and I left to start packing.

"*Wow,*" I thought.

I'm normally a positive, can do, kind of guy. But, I immediately had serious concerns.

All I could think about was, "Did this woman really know anything about warfare or Command and Control? Maybe she had been in the military. If so, it couldn't have been for more than one enlistment. Even if she did, you learn nothing in your first enlistment. Besides this, she was managing it from Chesapeake, Virginia? How could this be anything but a disaster? I'm afraid I have my first bad assignment in the Navy. Oh well, we'll see."

I decided the only thing to do was make the best of it.

Brown Field California

On May 7, 2012, I reported to the duty officer the Office of Technology, Innovation and Acquisition (OTIA), Brown Field California around 1400 hours as Thomas Bennett in civilian clothes.

Brown Field was old naval air field located near the Mexican border South of San Diego. That made it near enough for me to live at home and commute to work.

After checking in, I was given an envelope, told that a driver will give me a tour of the base and then take me to my quarters.

At that precise moment, a young seaman said, "My name is Seaman Josh White, sir. Right this way, sir," He gathered up my belongings, and we left.

The driver showed me the Bachelor Officer's Quarters (BOQ), the gas station, Navy Exchange, Officer's Mess, then to the flight line. On the way back to the BOQ, I told the driver, "Drop me at the Officer's Club, and I'll walk to the BOQ from there."

I checked out the Officer's Club, had a beer, and then walked to my quarters. After getting comfortable, I opened the envelope that was given to me when I reported. It contained a single sheet of paper that read;

Briefing tomorrow 19 June 2012 @ 0800 hours
Conference room 1, Headquarters Building

The next day, I had breakfast and proceeded to the headquarters building.

I entered the conference room that was already filling with men and women. Each place at the conference table had an envelope with names on it. I found my name and sat down.

Unsure of who knew what, I introduced myself to my immediate table neighbors and said nothing more. The others coming later did likewise. We waited for a few minutes, and then an Admiral entered the room and went to the front position of the table.

He announced, "Good morning ladies and gentlemen."

We all said, "Good morning."

"Welcome to Brown Field. I am Rear Admiral James Murphy. As you know, you have all been assigned here as a part this, joint civilian-Government project.

You have all been carefully selected because of your record of successfully completing assignments coupled with your special experience on this program.

It is important, however, for you to know that your clearance still limits your exposure to a need to know basis only. While here, you are not to discuss your job or activities with anyone not part of your assigned group. Just know that all of you are in the same boat so keeping things to yourself will be understood by all.

The envelopes before you contain directions to your work areas. You will be met there and further indoctrinated. You are to proceed to your work area now. You are all dismissed except Thomas Bennett. Mr. Bennett, will you come with me please?"

I followed him to an office where I sat in a chair facing him. He extended his hand and I shook it.

He said, "We are happy to have you here. I just wanted to say that I will give you any support you might need. I would also like to invite you to my home for dinner as soon as you get settled in. Would this Friday be OK?"

"Friday would be fine," I replied.

Admiral Murphy then said, "Your office is in this building. I'll walk you over and introduce you to your staff."

We entered the office area where three people were at their desks.

Admiral Murphy announced, "Good morning. I would like to introduce you to Thomas Bennett. He is the project leader for the testing phase here at Brown Field."

We all shook hands and Meg Johnson, my new Administrative Assistant, asked, "Coffee, Mister Bennett?"

"Yes, but please call me Tom. And I'll take it black please," I said.

Meg brought my coffee and said, "We have an introduction meeting set up after lunch, if that's OK."

I said, "Fine. Could we have lunch together so we can get acquainted in a less formal setting?"

"I'd like that," she replied.

Over lunch, I learned she was married with a son and daughter. Meg's husband was a Navy Chief stationed at Brown Field.

After lunch, I went to the conference room for my briefing. I was met by a man named Adam Parish.

He introduced me and turned the meeting over to Ryan Bentley. Ryan gave an overview of the project objectives then said, "Each section leader will now present his or her status report."

"The first is Jeff Davis, Multitronics' Assistant Project Leader," Jeff then gave his briefing on the main analysis section.

The other team members, one by one, introduced themselves and gave his or her presentation.

The balance of the team was a cadre of eight military and Homeland Security experts as test monitors. Needless to say, my head was spinning. Lunch was brought in, and the briefings continued as we ate.

The briefings were finally finished around three-thirty in the afternoon. I was then given an envelope marked "Top Secret" and told to study the material on the disk as soon as possible. It was complete dossiers on every team member.

We all left for the Officer's Club for happy hour to get acquainted one on one. After about an hour, I excused myself and went home. I was anxious to start reading the dossiers until dinner.

When I got home, I saw a message light flashing on the phone. I immediately listened to the message.

The message said, "Hi, this is Mary. Please call me when you get back from dinner no matter what time it is."

I looked at my watch to see what time it was in Virginia. It was a quarter past nine. I dialed and she answered. "Hi Tom, may I call you Tom?"

I don't know why I was surprised that she knew who was calling but I was.

I said, "Hi. Tom will be fine."

Mary said, "Well, I imagine you've had a pretty full day? How are you holding up?"

I replied, "OK, but it was a bit overwhelming."

Mary said, "Enjoy it, tomorrow will be really busy."

I laughed and said, "Where do I get off this train?"

Mary said, "You can't. You're stuck and the doors are jammed. I know you've had a lot to absorb in one day. The days will be long, but the good side is, you get weekends off. Well, at least after a couple weeks."

I said, "Gee thanks. How do I rate such special favors?"

Mary said, "Oh, that's easy. Don't let this go to your head, but don't you know you are a special guy."

I said, "Thanks again, but why do I get the feeling another shoe is about fall."

"You never know do you?" she laughed.

I thought, *"Well at least Mary seems to have a good sense of humor."*

She was also easy to talk with and her voice and manner seemed familiar. Because of this I opened my big mouth before I engaged my brain, a very unusual thing for me to do.

I said, "I don't mind telling you that I am a little intimidated by being in charge of such a distinguished group of experts."

Mary said, in a serious tone, "Remember you are also the best in your area of expertise. You've got a pretty impressive resume you know. Just for the record, I can't see you being intimidated by anything or anyone. Everyone on the team has already read your dossier. We have all approved your selection to the team including your position as leader. Do you know that your selection has also been blessed by the Joint Chiefs of Staff, the Multitronics CEO, and the President himself?"

I said, "Yes, I do."

Mary said, "Please call me in the morning right after breakfast and before you get to the office. I would like these nightly calls to be our daily routine for a while. Is that OK with you?" she asked.

I said, "Yes," and we ended our first conversation.

The next morning, I dressed and went to the office to start my first day. I had a lot to think about as I recalled yesterday's briefing. I was still overwhelmed.

I grabbed a cup of coffee and sat down at my desk. I found my e-mail full and my "In" basket overflowing. I began to read my e-mails. About 5 minutes later, there was a knock on the door.

"Enter," I said.

It was Ryan Bentley.

He asked, "How are you this morning?"

I said, "Very well, considering I haven't had a good night's sleep yet."

Ryan replied. "Welcome to the club. No rest for the weary. You might as well get your feet wet so here goes."

He reviewed a variety of issues and left.

The phone then began to ring, and I was on the phone with various people until lunch. I still hadn't read my e-mails, or anything from my "In" basket and didn't for the rest of the day. The "In" basket and e-mails just kept piling up. At the end of the day, I put the laptop and stuff from the "In" basket into my briefcase and headed for home. I got home, and saw the phone message flashing.

The message said, "Hi, if you are home before dinner, call me before you go to eat."

I called Mary, and we talked for about half an hour. This routine continued for the next two weeks.

Mary would always begin with, "Anything happen today that we need to discuss?"

If yes, we discussed it, and if no, we just chatted about nothing for about half an hour. After dinner, I read the personal dossiers, usually one each night. It was a few weeks before I finally got a break from the early to rise and late to bed routine.

One evening after my regularly scheduled phone call to Mary, I had dinner and a couple of drinks at the Officer's Club. I drove home to find my message light flashing again.

The message said, "Hi, call me when you get home."

I looked at my watch. It was a little past seven o'clock. It was late but I thought it might be important so I dialed the phone.

After a few rings I heard her say, "Hi."

I said, "Hi. I hope it's not too late. What's up?"

Mary said, "No, I'm glad you called.

I have an important unscheduled meeting tomorrow and wanted to ask you a few questions just to make sure I'm prepared. First, I wanted to ask what your first impressions of the operation there and how you are doing? Second, I have some business specifics that I need your thoughts on."

I told her, "Everything seems to be going very well. I think we both have good and competent teams here. I don't think the project could be in better hands than these teams."

"From what I see in the reports and hear from my guys, things are settling into a routine with no major issues," Mary replied.

I said, "That's the way I see it as well."

Mary said, "I'm happy to hear that from your perspective. I just don't like surprises. I feel better now. Sorry to keep you up. I'd better hang up and let you relax before bedtime."

I said, "Good night."

Mary said, "Goodnight," and hung up.

I relaxed and watched TV for a while then went to bed and slept like a baby for the first time since I arrived.

As the team leader, I had to keep in close e-mail contact with Mary. I had been corresponding with her only a short time when, somehow, little personal things entered our e-mails. Over the course of time, the personal e-mails progressed to the point that we began e-mailing outside business hours. We seemed to just connect and our online relationship grew.

I was now developing strong feelings even though I never met her and I sensed that the feelings were mutual. My old problem raised its head again. My thoughts went straight back to Annie.

I wondered if I would ever get over Annie. Also, I couldn't understand the hold she continued to have over me. Oh well, I pushed Annie from my thoughts.

To my surprise, I began thinking about Mary. A thousand times, I imagined what she might look like but was always afraid to ask for her picture.

One night Mary shocked me by saying, "I think our relationship should go back to business only. Toward that end, I think we should cut back on our personal e-mails, and limit our personal phone calls. I think any personal relationship involves too high a risk. All I know about you is that you have a fictitious identity and are a naval officer.

I have already divulged more about my personal life and feelings than I have in a very long time. I'm very uncomfortable with that."

I told her, "I understand but as much as I don't want to, I guess I have to agree with you. However, I would like to address the risk part. I can tell you that I am not married and the only personal relationship with a female is with you. That should eliminate that risk."

We tried stopping personal e-mails and limiting personal calls, but we just couldn't stop our personal chats.

After a couple of days, I told Mary, "What the hell. I can't do this. I can't go to sleep if I don't talk to you at night."

Mary replied, "Same here. I've decided that it can't do any harm."

We talked every night before going to bed. These calls were always personal. We refused to discuss business at night from then on except at the end of every work day, I called Mary before dinner to quickly fill her in on anything I felt she should know. I was determined to not talk business in our after dinner conversations. This became our daily routine.

The Brown Field assignment would soon be over, and I would transfer back to Maryland. From there, I would be responsible for operational testing and training on the new Navy system at Naval Station Norfolk, Virginia.

Just before the project ended, I called Mary and said, "I want us to meet as soon as I get relocated."

Mary said, "I'd like that very much. Call me after you get settled."

"Great, that's a deal," I replied.

Mary said, "Tom, in all fairness to you, I have another big issue that you need to know about. So far in my life, no man has ever measured up with my first love. I just can't help myself so I think any relationship between us may have to be as just friends. I couldn't, in clear conscious, have any personal relationship with you without telling you that up front. If you can accept this, we can take the next step."

I replied, "I also have a confession. I too have a first love that haunts me to this day. She is out of my life, and I want to forget and move on with my life. I guess that puts us in the same boat, doesn't it?"

Mary said, "OK, now that we both put our cards on the table, I think we can take the next step."

I commented, "Your first love must have been one hell of a guy. That's a long time to carry a torch. I'm sure we both will, sooner or later, find someone and be happy."

It was then that I realized I hadn't thought about Annie once until this moment. I wondered if Annie would return to haunt me after I met Mary.

Project Completion

⚜

On August 29th, 2012 I walked briskly into the administration building and toward the cafeteria. I was smiling and cheerfully saying, "Good morning, good morning," to everyone I passed.

I had called the last meeting of the Quick Fox project team for 0800 hours in the cafeteria. I was already looking forward to the next phase of the program with anticipation. It was 0759 when I entered the room.

At the front of the room was a table with a microphone standing behind it. Behind the microphone was a large screen. On the table was a speaker telephone that was hooked into the PA system and a document.

Entering the room, I made my way to the microphone.

There were people sitting quietly, some were just milling around, and others were in small groups talking.

I tapped the mic and announced, "Attention. May I have your attention, please?"

When everyone was seated and quiet, I began, "Good morning. It is with a great sense of pride and satisfaction that I can tell you that the Quick Fox Acceptance Testing is successfully completed.

On behalf of the United States Joint Chiefs of Staff, I now formally sign the "Document of Acceptance." I then signed the document.

Immediately, there was applause and cheering.

I said, "Quiet please. Mary Jackson is holding on the phone and wants to say a few words. I pushed the button on the phone and said, "You're on Mary."

Mary said, "Good morning everyone. On behalf of Multitronics, I want to thank you all for an amazing job well done. As many of you know, I have been part of Project Quick Fox for my entire career. As a matter of fact, this project really began when I was around nine years old when I began to help dad with his model control units. This is a very emotional moment because I can't help thinking of my dad and how proud he would be of our achievement. Goodbye and I wish you all the best as you go into the future. Now please direct your attention to the screen at the front of the room."

The lights then dimmed and the screen lit up.

It was the President of the Unites States and he began speaking, "Good morning ladies and gentlemen. It is with a great sense of satisfaction that I speak to you today. This is truly an historic moment. This morning marks the successful end of ten years of development that could be more significant than our space program. I say that because this could end war forever. If not, it will certainly change the way war and small conflicts alike are conducted and will save countless lives. It will dramatically reduce civilian collateral casualties when armed conflicts become necessary. And, this will be for the betterment of all mankind.

Unfortunately, because of the high security of this program, your effort cannot be recognized publically for at least the next fifty years. However, it is my pleasure to award a special Presidential Achievement Commendation to each person that has participated in this program. This commendation will not specify what it's given for but each of you will know why.

On behalf of all Americans and our allies who participated, I congratulate you for a job well done. Thank you, goodbye, and good luck."

The screen went dark. A few seconds later the lights came on and General Mark James Bailey, Chairman of the Joint Chiefs of Staff, came to the microphone.

He opened, "Mary, Tom, ladies and gentlemen. I would like to add my congratulations for an excellent job. I believe this is a turning point in history, and someday your descendants can be told that each of you contributed to the betterment of mankind.

As for the future, many of you will now proceed to the final phase of the program. The plan is to have all military and civilian systems fully operational within five years.

Now is the end of the beginning, and the beginning of a better future. We can all look forward to a safer, and better world thanks to all that made this possible. I'll conclude by simply adding my thank you."

There was silence for a few seconds. One person began to slowly clap their hands. Then others began to clap, a few at a time until all bedlam broke out. Cheers abounded and everyone was standing, hugging, and back slapping.

I finally said, "Can I have your attention please?"

Again, I knocked on the table and announced, "Attention please."

They all sat down.

I said, "I have one other announcement."

The room became quiet and I said, "It is my pleasure to announce that, at seven o'clock this morning the Multitronics Board of Directors unanimously voted to appoint Mary as its new President and Chief Executive Officer replacing Bob Andrews who has been appointed Chairman of the Board. Let's give her a big and well deserved hand."

Once again, there was applause and congratulations.

Mary said, "Thank you and I wish you all a happy and prosperous future. Goodbye for now."

I then dismissed the meeting and walked back to my office. I would, at long last, finally return to a regular Navy assignment whatever it might be. There sure has been a lot of water under the bridge in my life up to this point. I was looking forward to learning what my next assignment would be.

My mind was now wandering between Becky and Mary. It seems my conscience was working overtime. The last time I was with Becky, I concluded that we would get together and, maybe, get married. Why wasn't I in more of a hurry to see her? I wondered, *"What in the hell is wrong with me? I shouldn't be going to meet Mary with potentially having a relationship on my mind. I've got to make up my damned mind!"*

Now, I decided that since I had already made a date to meet Mary, I would go ahead and meet her, then go see Becky the following week. I would just tell Mary the truth.

Then, I would go see Becky and begin our future together.

Besides that, Mary and I only have a telephone relationship, even if it was very good.

"OK, I feel better after now."

Tom and Mary Meet

fter the meeting at Brown Field, I got a surprise. Mary called and said, "The Company just told me that I was going to personally oversee the operational testing phase.

She said, "Our meeting in person would be unavoidable now even if we tried because we will be working together. Besides that, I'm ready to meet you in person. We seem so compatible and our relationship is so natural that I'm really ready to chance it."

I said, "Wonderful, I can't wait."

Mary asked, "When do you arrive?"

"I report to Norfolk on Wednesday, October 1st."

She asked, "Can you barbeque?"

I said, "They don't call me Chef Bennett for nothing."

"Good, would you like to come to my house for a barbeque on Sunday?"

I immediately said, "Yes."

Mary said, "Don't forget to bring your swim suit. I have a nice pool."

I was pleased but felt a little guilty leaving the impression that we might continue our relationship.

"Didn't I just decide to go to Becky? As fickle as I am, I should stay out of a relationship with both of them. Boy, Annie sure fucked me up. I'll just have to decide, once and for all."

I reported in at the Naval Research Labs on October 2nd and was given my next assignment. It seems that I would have two jobs. In addition to my regular job, I would become involved with Afghanistan again. The President has appointed me Special Envoy to Afghanistan.

The U.S. Forces were being reduced and would be completely out of Afghanistan by the end of 2014. The President's plan was to reinforce the CIA and Special Forces before the troops are withdrawn. We had to do something to ensure the Taliban didn't come back in and take control of the country again.

To that end, I was ordered to work with my old friend Maryam Alizai to expand the HER, building a wide spread intelligence presence throughout Afghanistan and Pakistan.

When I arrived at my new office, I saw a familiar face. It was Basira Zazi from Afghanistan. Only now, she was Basira Monroe. She had been our Administrative Assistant in Jalalabad. Now she was my personal assistant. It was obvious she didn't recognize me.

After all, it was five years later and I was in uniform, a long way from what I looked like then. She showed me around and I said nothing. After I got back to my desk, I pushed the intercom button.

Basira answered, "Yes sir, Captain."

I replied, in Pashto "Please come into the office."

"Yes sir. Do I need to bring anything?"

"No," I replied.

She entered the office and said, "You speak Farsi very well. Where did you learn it?"

I said, "Look at me carefully. Look at my eyes. Don't you recognize me?"

"No sir. Should I recognize you?"

I replied, "You knew me very well. You helped me a lot in Afghanistan.

"I can't believe that!" she said.

"You know me as Abdul Rahid," I said.

"No way." she said.

I went around the desk, gave her a big hug and asked, "Do you know me now?"

She was still in disbelief but said, "I guess so but you sure look different. Are you sure?"

I laughed and said, "Yes, it's really me,"

We then spent the next hour catching each other up with the latest.

Basira had married an American Officer, James Monroe and immigrated to the U.S. three years ago. She was assigned to me because we had worked together, plus she was very well known and trusted by our people in Afghanistan.

Lastly, she told me that I was already scheduled to go to Afghanistan in January. There I would meet with none other than Maryam and Begom Jan. My head was now spinning like a top wondering where the next assignment would take me.

Sunday came and it was time to go to Mary's. I jumped on Old Harley and headed for Mary's. In the meantime, Mary was in the kitchen literally pacing back and forth.

Mary's Mom asked, "What's the matter, honey?"

Mary said, "I feel like there is going to be a train wreck, and I'm standing in the middle of the tracks.

I've allowed myself to develop strong feelings for a man I've never even seen, let alone met. How could I have done that? I've imagined this great looking knight in shining armor riding a black stallion. He told me he rode a black motorcycle, not a black stallion. What if he is actually a "Biker" with tattoos all over his body and long hair and a beard? His face could even be scarred from street fights."

Mom quickly replied, "Wow. Your imagination sure is running wild. I can't believe you. Does he talk like a biker?"

Mary said, "No, he is soft spoken, educated, and considerate."

"Mom replied, "See, he couldn't be like a biker like you envision. I think he will be as good looking and charming as you imagine."

Mary said, "Oh my God, that would be worse."

Mom asked, "How on earth would that be bad?"

"My relationship destroyer Randy, that's how.

I can see it now. I can just imagine that he will come in and be all that I had hoped for, then 'that boy' will ruin it before the day is over. I don't think I could handle my emotions. I just feel I am setting myself up for another heart break. Maybe I should call and cancel."

Mom said, "It's too late now so just brace yourself. Everything will be OK no matter what happens. I have a good feeling about this."

"I sure hope you are right about him, I can hardly stand it. Well, we'll just have to take it a step at a time. Who knows, we might not even like each other after getting acquainted."

Mom said, "That's right, just be yourself and play it by ear. After all, you are the President of a major corporation. You can surely handle this."

"OK Mom, when he gets here, would you answer the door while I go freshen up before we meet?"

In the meantime, I was now riding up Interstate 264 on my Harley headed for Mary's.

On the way, I wondered, *"What would she look like? What would she be like in person? What if Mary was ugly? After all, she was thirty four, unmarried and still living with her mother. Maybe she looked like the wicked witch from the East."*

Then, I thought about her son. Mary had told me how he destroyed every relationship she ever tried to have.

I imagined this obnoxious fourteen year old menace out to torpedo everything.

I'm wondering, *"What am I getting myself into. Maybe I should call Mary and cancel. I could say some emergency came up. But I was so close to her house now and canceling would be rude. It was too late now. I'll just play it by ear and let the chips fall where they fall."*

A few minutes later I arrived and rang the doorbell.

The door opened and a nice looking older woman said, "You must be Tom. I'm Dorothy. We've talked on the phone. I'm pleased to finally meet you. Mary has told me so much about you. I feel I already know you."

Dorothy led me to the living room and said, "Please have a seat. Mary will out in a couple of minutes."

I just stood there looking around. The house was beautiful. The living room was to the right and sunken. As I entered the living room, there was a massive fireplace on the right side of the room and in the far left corner was a baby grand piano. Over the fireplace was a large portrait of Rembrandt's *"The Man in the Golden Helmet."*

On the wall next to the piano was another large painting. It was Monet's *"Red Boats at Argenteuil"* I just stood there waiting.

Mary quickly checked and touched up her makeup, straightened her clothes, and went to the living room. She saw a tall man in front of the fireplace talking to her Mom.

As she got closer Mary thought, *"I can't believe my eyes. Oh my God, it looks like Jim!"*

I stopped and just stood there looking at him trying to see if it really was him. Still thinking it was him, I said, "I think the moon has turned to blue cheese."

When I heard those words I thought, *"Could that be Annie?"*

I immediately turned around and saw that it really was Annie.

"Does that mean I can kiss you?" I asked.

"No. That means you had damned well better kiss me."

Annie ran as fast as she could with her arms wide open.

We hugged each other, and then both pulled our heads back to look into each other's eyes.

Annie said, "I'm soooo happy, but I'm so totally confused and bewildered."

Annie thought, "*My God, I'm swooning and think my knees will collapse. That same feeling is still there just as it was on the cruise.*"

Tom finally said, "I'll tell you everything I can. I then noticed that Mary and Dorothy kept looking at me and back at each other with a strange look on their faces.

Finally, Dorothy said, "Annie, you've got to tell him."

"Tell me what?" I asked.

After a short pause, Mary said, "There's only one way to do this so here goes, I've got a big secret to tell you and she paused again."

Then she said, "You have a son."

I was stunned.

Before I could say anything, Randy came in, looked at me and said, "Hi Jon, I didn't know you were coming."

Surprised, Mary asked, "How do you know him? Why did you call him Jon?"

Randy replied, "He is my friend from Pasadena. He was my baseball coach. He promised he would come see me."

Dorothy then said, "Boy, what a small world."

Mary then said, "Randy, I've got something to tell you. Randy, Jon is your father."

Before I could say anything Randy asked, "You are my real Dad?"

All I could say is, "That's what your mother said."

Mary said, "Yes, he really is. Shall we keep him?"

Randy didn't answer, but ran and put his arms around my neck. In his usual vernacular, Randy just said, "Cool. Way cool."

Mary, Randy, and I just stood in a group hug, and no one said anything for a long time.

Dorothy finally said, "This is what I call a happily ever after story if I ever heard one," and joined the group hug.